Y

THE LAST MAN

Book Two

Brian K. Vaughan Writer

Pia Guerra, Goran Parlov, Paul Chadwick Pencillers

José Marzán, Jr. Inker

Pamela Rambo, Zylonol Colorists

Clem Robins Letterer

J.G. Jones, Aron Wiesenfeld,
Massimo Carnevale Original Series Covers

Y: THE LAST MAN created by Brian K. Vaughan and Pia Guerra

Steve Bunche, Will Dennis Editors – Original Series
Zachary Rau, Casey Seijas Assistant Editors – Original Series
Jeb Woodard Group Editor – Collected Editions
Scott Nybakken Editor – Collected Edition
Steve Cook Design Director – Books
Louis Prandi Publication Design
Shelly Bond VP & Executive Editor – Vertigo
Diane Nelson President
Dan DiDio and Jim Lee Co-Publishers
Geoff Johns Chief Creative Officer
Amit Desai Senior VP – Marketing & Global Franchise Management
Nairi Gardiner Senior VP – Finance
Sam Ades VP – Digital Marketing
Bobbie Chase VP – Talent Development
Mark Chiarello Senior VP – Art, Design & Collected Editions
John Cunningham VP – Content Strategy
Anne DePies VP – Strategy Planning & Reporting
Don Falletti VP – Manufacturing Operations
Lawrence Ganem VP – Editorial Administration & Talent Relations
Alison Gill Senior VP – Manufacturing & Operations
Hank Kanalz Senior VP – Editorial Strategy & Administration
Jay Kogan VP – Legal Affairs
Derek Maddalena Senior VP – Sales & Business Development
Jack Mahan VP – Business Affairs
Dan Miron VP – Sales Planning & Trade Development
Nick Napolitano VP – Manufacturing Administration
Carol Roeder VP – Marketing
Eddie Scannell VP – Mass Account & Digital Sales
Courtney Simmons Senior VP – Publicity & Communications
Jim (Ski) Sokolowski VP – Comic Book Specialty & Newsstand Sales
Sandy Yi Senior VP – Global Franchise Management

Cover illustration by Massimo Carnevale.
Logo design by Terry Marks.

Y: THE LAST MAN
BOOK TWO

Published by DC Comics.
Compilation Copyright © 2015 Brian K. Vaughan and Pia Guerra.
All Rights Reserved. Cover Copyright © 2009 DC Comics.
All Rights Reserved. Script Copyright © 2003 Brian K. Vaughan and Pia Guerra.
All Rights Reserved.

Originally published in single magazine form as Y: THE LAST MAN 11-23. Copyright © 2003, 2004 Brian K. Vaughan and Pia Guerra. All Rights Reserved. All characters, their distinctive likenesses and related elements featured in this publication are trademarks of Brian K. Vaughan and Pia Guerra. VERTIGO is a trademark of DC Comics. The stories, characters and incidents featured in this publication are entirely fictional. DC Comics does not read or accept unsolicited submissions of ideas, stories or artwork.

DC Comics, 2900 W. Alameda Avenue, Burbank, CA 91505 Printed by Transcontinental Interglobe Beauceville, Canada. Second Printing. ISBN: 978-1-4012-5439-1

Library of Congress Cataloging-in-Publication Data

Vaughan, Brian K, author.
Y, the last man. Book two / Brian K. Vaughan, Pia Guerra, José Marzán, Jr., Goran Parlov.
pages cm
"Originally published in single magazine form as Y: The Last Man 11-23."
ISBN 978-1-4012-5439-1
1. Graphic novels. I. Guerra, Pia, illustrator. II. Marzán, José, illustrator. III. Parlov, Goran, illustrator. IV. Title.
PN6728.Y2V45 2013
741.5'973—dc23
2013011671

FSC
www.fsc.org

MIX
Paper from responsible sources
FSC® C011825

Y: THE LAST MAN — Contents

Marquand, Missouri
Now

WHAT KIND OF SOMETHING?

HALF A PACK.

WHEN THE HELL DID YOU START *SMOKING*, 355?

WHEN A PLAGUE OF BIBLICAL PROPORTIONS KILLED EVERY MAN EXCEPT FOR *YOUR* HAIRY ASS?

FAIR ENOUGH.

CAN I BUM ONE OFF YOU?

SORRY, 'RICK. THE PRESIDENT ORDERED ME TO *PROTECT* YOU, NOT TO SULLY YOUR PINK LUNGS.

SUIT YOURSELF.

HOPE THE CULPER RING TAUGHT YOU HOW TO RUB TWO STICKS TOGETHER.

IF YOU EVER TELL YOUR MOTHER ABOUT THIS, I'LL KILL YOU MYSELF.

GOD YOU'RE EASY...

"FUCK COMMUNISM"?

WHAT ARE YOU, A COSSACK?

OH, THE ENGRAVING?

IT'S FROM THIS THING I READ BACK IN HIGH SCHOOL, A, UH...A "GRAPHIC NOVEL." YOU KNOW, LIKE A COMIC BOOK?

THEY CAN SAY "FUCK" IN COMIC BOOKS?

I GUESS.

JEEZ, THEY NEVER SAID STUFF LIKE THAT IN *SUPERMAN*.

SUPERMAN'S JUST MAKE-BELIEVE, 355.

IN THE REAL WORLD...

RELAX, DOC, IT'S JUST--

WHATEVER, BREAK'S OVER. THEY'VE APPARENTLY FINISHED REPAIRING THE LITTLE ENGINE THAT COULDN'T.

AND GET THIS ANIMAL AWAY FROM ME. IT DEFECATED IN MY *MEDICAL BAG.*

COME ON, AMPERSAND...BEFORE MRS. HYDE'S TRANSFORMATION IS COMPLETE.

GO EASY ON HIM, DR. MANN. HE'S STILL NOT OVER WHAT HAPPENED BACK IN MARRISVILLE.

355, IS THERE SOMETHING GOING *ON* BETWEEN YOU TWO?

WHO, ME AND...?

EW, NO!

THIS ISN'T *POST-COITAL,* IF THAT'S WHAT YOU'RE SUGGESTING.

WELL, IT'S JUST...BACK IN OHIO, YOU *SAID* SOMETHING. WHEN YOU WERE UNCONSCIOUS. YOU SAID...

FORGET IT.

PROBABLY JUST THE ANESTHESIA TALKING.

TRUST ME, DOCTOR, MY ONLY INTEREST IN YORICK IS KEEPING HIM OUT OF *TROUBLE...*

12

SO, YOU GOT A GIRL-FRIEND?

OR ARE YOU A WORKING GIRL LIKE ME?

GIRLFRIEND.

WE'RE ENGAGED, ACTUALLY... MORE OR LESS.

GOOD, I WAS AFRAID YOU WERE GONNA TAKE ALL OF MY CUSTOMERS ON THIS LINE.

SERIOUSLY, YOUR LADY'S LUCKY TO HAVE SOMEONE AS DEDICATED AS YOU. BIND THOSE BREASTS A LITTLE TIGHTER AND YOU'LL ALMOST BE PASSABLE.

...THANKS?

ANYWAY, HAVE A SAFE TRIP,

KEEP AN EYE OUT FOR AMAZONS!

WILL DO.

YOU AND ME, LITTLE BUDDY...ADRIFT IN AN OCEAN OF ESTROGEN.

ER AH HA

ROCKS AND TREES, ROCKS AND TREES...

I CAN'T WAIT TO GET OUT OF THIS GODDAMN CABOOSE FOR GOOD.

DON'T GET TOO EXCITED, YORICK. EVEN WHEN WE *DO* REACH SAN FRANCISCO, IT'S NOT LIKE WE'LL HAVE TIME FOR CRACKED CRAB AND JET SKIS.

I HAVE HUNDREDS OF TESTS TO PERFORM ON YOU...PRESUMING MY LATE DAUGHTER'S EMBRYONIC CELLS ARE STILL INTACT FOR COMPARISON.

DAUGHTER? I THOUGHT THE CLONE YOU GAVE BIRTH TO WAS A *MALE.*

WHAT?

OF COURSE. THAT'S WHAT I--

THUNK

THE HELL...?

15

SOUNDS LIKE SOMETHING HIT OUR ROOF.

I'LL CHECK IT OUT.

I'M COMING WITH YOU.

NO!

IF HE TRIES TO FOLLOW ME, DO WHAT WE DISCUSSED.

I'M ON IT.

WHAT THE FUCK?

OH, YOU GUYS STINK.

IF ANYBODY'S THERE, I'M COMING UP!

AND I'M ARMED!

NO! PLEASE!

IT TOOK ME DAYS TO GET BACK ON TRAIN! I AM TRYING TO GET TO MAN!

USE MY HELP, PLEASE!

I SAVE LIFE AND YOU LET ME INSIDE YOUR TRAIN, DA?

THAT MEDAL... HOW THE HELL DID YOU GET A GOLD STAR?

I WAS GOOD LITTLE GIRL IN SCHOOL.

BUT THAT'S RESERVED FOR HEROES OF THE RUSSIAN FEDERA--

NO MORE KICKING, NO MORE QUESTIONS. WE ARE FRIENDS AND EVEN, OKAY?

355!

UM... EVERYTHING COOL UP HERE?

GODDAMMIT, YORICK.

HOW...?

HEY, I RECOGNIZE HER.

SHE'S THAT STOWAWAY THEY THREW OFF THE TRAIN BACK IN MARRISVILLE.

WHO... WHO IS THIS MAN?

HE'S NOT THE PERSON YOU'RE AFTER?

NO, I AM GOING TO KANSAS FOR...FOR...

IT IS VERY HARD TO BE EXPLAINING FOR ME IN YOUR LANGUAGE.

⟨THEN TRY IT IN YOUR TONGUE.⟩

⟨YOU SPEAK RUSSIAN?⟩

⟨NOT FOR LONG TIME.⟩

⟨MY GRAMMAR IS A LITTLE, UM... FROGGY?⟩

22

‹THANK CHRIST! I SOUND LIKE A FUCKING *RETARD* WHEN I TRY TO SPEAK ENGLISH.›

‹SLOW DOWN. WHO *IS* YOU?›

‹MY NAME'S NATALYA ZAMYATIN.›

‹I WAS SENT BY WHAT'S LEFT OF THE GOVERNMENT TO RETRIEVE OUR COUNTRY'S ONLY LIVING MALE, A COSMONAUT ON BOARD THE INTERNATIONAL SPACE STATION.›

‹WHAT?›

HEY, COMRADES, CAN SOMEONE TRANSLATE THIS OR--

‹FOR MONTHS, HE'S BEEN TRAPPED INSIDE THE I.S.S. WITH TWO OF YOUR ASTRONAUTS, ONE MALE AND ONE FEMALE.›

‹HOW CAN YOU BE SURE HE'S STILL ALIVE?›

‹WELL, WE LOST HAM CONTACT A FEW WEEKS AGO, BUT MY PEOPLE HAVE TALKED TO BOTH MEN SINCE JULY, SO WE KNOW THEY SURVIVED THE PLAGUE.›

‹THEY'VE BEEN WAITING FOR *NASA* TO SEND A SHUTTLE TO RESCUE THEM...BUT HOUSTON APPARENTLY DOESN'T HAVE THE RESOURCES TO MAKE THAT HAPPEN.›

‹THEN HOW ARE *YOU* PLANNING TO GET UP THERE?›

‹I'M NOT.›

‹THEY'RE COMING DOWN HERE.›

YOU'VE HEARD THE HORROR STORIES, RIGHT? THE SOYUZ ISN'T A LIFE-BOAT, IT'S A *DEATHTRAP.*

WELL, WE'RE OBVIOUSLY NOT BEING SENT THAT LIMO WE REQUESTED, AND I'D RATHER BITE IT IN SOME CORNFIELD THAN SUFFOCATE INSIDE THIS *JUNKHEAP.*

EVEN IF WE *DON'T* CRASH, HOW CAN WE BE SURE THAT WHATEVER KILLED ALL THE MEN DOWN THERE WON'T KILL *YOU* THE SECOND WE LAND?

WE CAN'T, BUT WE'RE TAKING EVERY PRECAUTION POSSIBLE, CIBA.

WE'RE GOING DOWN IN SUITS, AND VLAD'S CONTACT IS SUPPOSED TO BE WAITING AT OUR E.L.Z. TO ESCORT US TO THE HOT SUITE AS SOON AS WE BLOW THE LATCH.

TRUE, COMMANDER...

...BUT FIRST WE MUST SURVIVE REENTRY.

SPEED LIMIT 1750

28 MILL

VLAD. SORRY, I THOUGHT YOU WERE STILL IN THE HEAD, TRIMMING THAT NEW SOUP STRAINER OF YOURS.

LISTEN, WHAT I WAS SAYING... IT HAS NOTHING TO DO WITH MY FAITH IN YOU AS A PILOT.

NOR SHOULD IT BE MY *ABILITIES* WHICH CONCERN YOU.

BECAUSE OF CHEMICAL DEGRADATION IN HYDRAZINE FUEL, SOYUZ WAS DESIGNED TO BE STORED IN SPACE FOR MAXIMUM OF SIX MONTHS.

OUR VESSEL HAS NOT BEEN REPLACED IN MORE THAN *NINE.*

SURE, BUT WE'VE GOT SOME WIGGLE ROOM WITH THOSE NUMBERS, RIGHT?

RUSSIAN ENGINEERS ARE NOT BIG ON "WIGGLE ROOM," SIR.

SO HOW CAN WE TELL IF THE PROPELLANT'S CORRODED ANY OF OUR SOYUZ'S DEEP PLUMBING?

ONLY ONE WAY TO KNOW FOR CERTAIN...

...IF OUR CABIN BURSTS INTO FLAMES WHEN WE ENTER ATMOSPHERE.

THIS JUST KEEPS GETTING BETTER AND BETTER...

25

Marquand, Missouri
Two Hours Later

DID YOU KNOW SHAKESPEARE COINED THAT PHRASE?

WHAT?

"WILD-GOOSE CHASE," I MEAN.

ORIGINALLY, IT DESCRIBED AN UNPREDICTABLE PATH TAKEN BY ONE INDIVIDUAL AND FOLLOWED BY ANOTHER...ENDING WHEN THE FIRST IS INEVITABLY *CAUGHT*.

MY SPOUSE LOVED TO POINT OUT THAT ITS MODERN USAGE IS REALLY A PESSIMISTIC MISINTERPRETATION OF--

ENOUGH! FOR MONTHS, YOU HAVE BORED ME WITH THIS PEDANTIC NONSENSE, WHILE GIVING ME NO *USEFUL* INFORMATION. I HAVE YET TO EVEN LEARN YOUR REAL NAME *!*

ALTER, BE PATIENT. I'VE TOLD YOU EVERYTHING YOU NEED TO KNOW TO FIND THE LAST MAN ON EARTH, AND YOU'RE *CLOSE*.

I'M NOT SURE HOW SECURE THIS FREQUENCY IS, SO I CAN'T SAY MORE THAN--

THAT EXCUSE IS NO LONGER ACCEPTABLE. GIVE ME A REASON TO CONTINUE TRUSTING YOU, OR I AM TAKING MY TROOPS BACK TO TEL AVIV.

NOW, FOR THE LAST TIME, WHO *ARE* YOU?

GOOD LORD, ISN'T IT *OBVIOUS*, ALTER?

THE LAST MAN ON EARTH IS YOUR *CHILD?*

UNLESS I *IMAGINED* THOSE TWENTY-SIX HOURS I WAS IN LABOR.

MY NAME IS REPRESENTATIVE JENNIFER BROWN. I'M--

REPRESENTATIVE? YOU'RE A U.S. *CONGRESSWOMAN?* THEN, WHY THE HELL DID YOU ASK *ISRAEL* FOR HELP? YOUR OWN MILITARY IS--

--STILL IN DISARRAY, ALTER, AS YOU'VE SEEN. I KNEW *YOU* WERE THE ONLY WOMAN WITH THE SKILLS AND RESOURCES TO RETRIEVE MY SON.

YOUR PREDECESSOR WAS...HE WAS A DEAR *FRIEND* OF MINE. LIEUTENANT-GENERAL YEHUDA ALWAYS SPOKE VERY HIGHLY OF YOU.

BESIDES, I'VE RUN OUT OF *AMERICANS* I CAN TRUST.

EXPLAIN.

I ASSURE YOU, THE NETWORK MY PEOPLE CREATED IS SECURE. OUR FREQUENCY IS--

YES, YES, FINE. IT HAPPENED SHORTLY AFTER MY SON LEFT WASHINGTON...

I LEARNED THE ORGANIZATION THAT HAD SWORN TO *PROTECT* YORICK WASN'T MADE UP OF ALTRUISTIC SERVANTS OF THE EXECUTIVE BRANCH, AS OUR NEW PRESIDENT HAD LED ME TO BELIEVE.

THIS "CULPER RING" IS ACTUALLY A GROUP OF THUGS AND... AND *ASSASSINS*, A GLORIFIED DIRTY TRICKS CREW. FOR DECADES, THEY'VE COMMITTED ATROCITIES FOR CORRUPT ADMINISTRATIONS.

AND YOU NOW SUSPECT THAT THIS GROUP HAS, WHAT, *KIDNAPPED* YOUR SON?

ONE OF THEIR AGENTS, YES... "355." I'M NOT SURE WHAT HER AGENDA IS, BUT I KNOW THAT SHE RECENTLY TRANSPORTED YORICK TO YOUR CURRENT LOCATION.

YOU ORIGINALLY SAID THEY WERE LOOKING FOR SOME GENETICIST IN *BOSTON*. WHAT MAKES YOU THINK YOUR SON AND HIS CAPTOR ARE NOW HERE IN *MISSOURI*?

THERE'S A CHANCE THEY MAY HAVE JUST BEEN PASSING THROUGH, ALTER. SEE, AN ASSOCIATE IN THE SECRET SERVICE ENCOURAGED ME TO PLANT A *TRACKING DEVICE* ON YORICK BEFORE HE LEFT.

WITH THE SATELLITES DOWN, SHE'S BEEN TRIANGULATING USING WHATEVER RADIO TOWERS ARE AVAILABLE, AND IT SOMETIMES TAKES A FEW *HOURS* TO GET A LOCK.

EITHER WAY, HOW CAN YOU BE CERTAIN THIS BEACON HASN'T BEEN FOUND AND REMOVED?

BECAUSE WE HID IT INSIDE YORICK'S MONKEY.

HIS *WHAT?*

31

Oldenbrook, Kansas
Ten Hours Later

IF WHAT NATALYA SAYS IS TRUE, A SOYUZ ESCAPE VESSEL IS ABOUT TO LAND WITH ONE FEMALE AND TWO MALES INSIDE. TWO *LIVING* MALES.

THOSE ASTRONAUTS ARE GOING TO NEED MY PROTECTION AND YOUR MEDICAL ATTENTION.

AND MY DISARMING WIT!

SERIOUSLY, DOC, LET YOUR UNFEELING CYBORG BRAIN RELEASE A LITTLE SEROTONIN FOR ONCE. THIS IS A MIRACLE!

NO, THIS IS A *SHAM.*

ANYONE WHO'S WATCHED AN HOUR'S WORTH OF DISCOVERY CHANNEL KNOWS THAT THE SOYUZ ALWAYS LANDS IN THE *KAZAKH STEPPES* OUTSIDE OF RUSSIA...

...NOT IN THE MIDDLE OF SOME ALFALFA FIELD IN BUMFUCK, KANSAS.

NO, KAZAKHSTAN IS *NO POSSIBLE!*

AKTAU MAKE *POISON!* AKTAU BRING DEATH!

WAIT, REWIND. WHAT'S *AKTAU?*

IT'S A NUCLEAR POWER PLANT.

NO. NOT ANOTHER *CHERNOBYL*.

WORSE. MY GOVERNMENT THINK POSSIBLE *ONE MILLION* WOMAN DEAD. NUMBERS WILL BECOME MORE WHEN CANCER BLOWS TO RUSSIA.

OF COURSE, IF I'M NO ABLE TO BRING BACK OUR COSMONAUT IN SAFETY, MY COUNTRY HAS MORE TO WORRY ABOUT FOR FUTURE THAN *DISEASE*.

‹NATALYA, I THOUGHT KAZAKHSTAN TOOK THEIR REACTOR, UM, WHAT'S THE RUSSIAN WORD FOR...?›

‹"OFFLINE"? YEAH, SO DID WE. BUT BEFORE THE PLAGUE, MALE OFFICIALS WERE APPARENTLY OPERATING IT IN SECRET FOR PROFIT.›

‹WHILE RUSSIA WAS WORKING ITS ASS OFF TO SHUT DOWN ALL OF OUR PLANTS, KAZAKHSTAN'S CORE WAS *MELTING DOWN*. ONE LAST "FUCK YOU" FROM A CORRUPT BUREAUCRACY.›

JESUS, WHAT A NIGHTMARE. ALL THOSE PEOPLE LIVED THROUGH THE PLAGUE...ONLY TO DIE IN SOME STUPID ACCIDENT?

IS HORRIBLE TRAGEDY, YES, BUT AT LEAST WOMEN HAD EACH OTHER, YORICK.

MY COUNTRY HAS SAYING, "EVEN DEATH IS BEAUTIFUL, IF YOU ARE NOT ALONE."

YOU SAY SO.

355, IF THAT HAPPENS TO ONE OF *OUR* REACTORS--

IT WON'T. MY COLLEAGUES HAVE BEEN DECOMMISSIONING PLANTS FOR MONTHS NOW, ALL ACROSS THE COUNTRY.

TRUST ME, THE CULPER RING IS TAKING CARE OF *EVERY-THING*.

International Space Station
Now

COMMANDER, YOU...YOU MUST FORGIVE ME.

I HAVE NO IDEA WHAT OVER-CAME ME.

YEAH, I'M I'M SORRY TOO, VLAD.

IT MUST BE THE OXYGEN DEPRIVATION, CIBA.

IT'S MAKING US PSYCHOTIC.

WELL, LET'S TRY TO KEEP IT TOGETHER, GENTLE-MEN. I KNOW IT FEELS LIKE WE'VE BEEN STUCK IN THIS THING TOGETHER FOREVER...

3,298 TRIPS AROUND THAT GOD-DAMN BLUE BALL.

TWICE AS MANY SHITTY POKER GAMES.

...BUT IN A FEW HOURS, IT'LL ALL BE OVER.

ONE WAY OR ANOTHER.

39

OKAY, BUT EVEN IF THESE THEORETICAL SPACEMEN REALLY *DID* ESCAPE THE PLAGUE, HOW DO WE KNOW IT WON'T AFFECT THEM ONCE THEY TOUCH DOWN?

WE DON'T. THIS IS WHY MY BOSSES ORDER SOYUZ TO LAND BY YOUR COUNTRY'S NEW, HOW DO YOU SAY...

IS IT "WARM ROOM"?

OUR *HOT SUITE?* THE RUSSIANS *KNEW* ABOUT IT?

K.G.B. IS DEAD, FRIEND, BUT OUR INTELLIGENCE IS NOT.

UM, I REALIZE MY USELESS B.A. IS SHOWING ...BUT WHAT THE HELL IS A HOT SUITE?

IT'S A GROUP OF LEVEL FOUR BIO-SAFETY ROOMS, SUPPOSEDLY IMPERVIOUS TO ANY INFECTIOUS AGENTS FROM THE OUTSIDE WORLD AND BLAH, BLAH, BLAH.

I KNEW THERE WAS ONE AT FORT DETRICK, BUT WE'RE IN THE MIDDLE OF *NOWHERE.*

THE GOVERNMENT HID A MASSIVE FACILITY OUT HERE FOR HIGH-RANKING OFFICIALS TO RETREAT TO IN CASE OF BIOLOGICAL ATTACKS TO MAJOR CITIES.

THEY *DID?* DO WE KNOW IF ANY DUDES WERE INSIDE THIS THING *BEFORE* THE PLAGUE HIT?

NOPE... BUT I GUESS WE'RE ABOUT TO FIND OUT.

VRRMM

‹FORGET ABOUT REFUELING, PILOT.›

‹WE'RE NOT FAR FROM THE NEW COORDINATES THE AMERICAN PROVIDED.›

‹MY, MISSOURI YESTERDAY AND KANSAS TODAY? LET US PRAY WE HAVE NOT ONCE AGAIN "NARROWLY MISSED" THE LAST BOY ON EARTH.›

‹SADIE, A MOMENT OF YOUR TIME, PLEASE.›

‹IF YOU EVER AGAIN TAKE THAT TONE WITH ME IN FRONT OF MY SOLDIERS...›

‹...I WILL HAVE TO ASK YOU TO STEP OUTSIDE.›

⟨I APOLOGIZE, LIEUTENANT-GENERAL, BUT I'M BEGINNING TO SUSPECT THAT YOU DRAGGED US ON THIS SCAVENGER HUNT SIMPLY BECAUSE YOU'D GROWN *BORED* WITH PEACE IN ISRAEL.⟩

⟨YOU'RE WRONG.⟩

⟨I'M DOING WHAT'S BEST FOR OUR PEOPLE.⟩

⟨WORKING AS AN ERRAND GIRL FOR SOME AMERICAN POLITICIAN?⟩

⟨NO, SEEING THAT THE ONLY FUNCTIONING *SPERM FACTORY* DOESN'T FALL INTO THE HANDS OF THE ENEMY.⟩

⟨YOU KEEP USING THAT TERM, "THE ENEMY."⟩

⟨BUT YOU TAUGHT ME THAT EUPHEMISMS ARE ONLY FOR THOSE WHO FEEL *GUILT* ABOUT WHAT THEY'RE DESCRIBING. IF YOUR CONSCIENCE IS CLEAR, ALTER, SAY WHAT YOU MEAN...⟩

⟨ARABS.⟩

‹THAT'S NOT WHAT THIS IS ABOUT. MY ONLY CONCERN IS *TERROR*. HAMAS, ISLAMIC JIHAD...›

‹THOSE GROUPS DON'T NEED *MEN* TO BLOW UP BUSES, ALTER! A...A *FEMALE* SUICIDE BOMBER KILLED MY BROTHER-IN-LAW!›

‹THEN YOU UNDER-STAND THE NEED FOR VIGILANCE.›

‹NO, I DON'T! THERE HASN'T BEEN A SINGLE BOMBING SINCE THE MEN DIED!›

‹AND I INTEND TO KEEP IT THAT WAY.›

‹HOW, BY REUNITING SOME RANDOM YOUNG MAN WITH HIS *MOTHER*?›

‹DON'T BE AN IDIOT, SADIE. I HAVE NO INTENTION OF RETURNING YORICK TO THAT GULLIBLE SIMPLETON.›

‹THE WAY SHE LOOKS AFTER HER SON, THAT WOULD BE TANTAMOUNT TO HANDING HIM DIRECTLY TO *HEZBOLLAH*.›

‹THEN...WHAT *ARE* YOU PLANNING TO DO WITH THE BOY?›

‹SET US DOWN HERE, PILOT.›

‹WE'LL GO IN THE REST OF THE WAY ON FOOT.›

‹IT'S IMPORTANT TO MAINTAIN THE ELEMENT OF SURPRISE.›

44

UM, WHY ARE YOU UNBUTTONING...?

YOUR COUNTRY SO BEAUTIFUL, BUT TOO FUCKING HOT.

ALWAYS THE HEAT...

NATALYA, I DON'T MEAN TO BE RUDE, BUT COULD YOU, UH, STAY AS CLOTHED AS POSSIBLE AROUND ME?

‹LORD, I NEVER THOUGHT I WOULD MISS MOSCOW.›

‹THE WAY THE MEN'S BODIES LITTERED RED SQUARE ...THEY LOOKED LIKE CHILDREN, MAKING ANGELS IN THE SNOW.›

‹AND I REMEMBER FINDING YOU, SWEET RODYA. THE IMAGE OF YOUR FACE, FROZEN IN MY MIND...›

ALSO, WOULD YOU MIND NOT MUTTERING TO YOURSELF IN RUSSIAN? YOUR ACCENT IS DISTURBINGLY SEXY.

IT'S JUST, I'VE GOT THIS GIRL I'M TRYING REALLY HARD TO STAY LOYAL TO, BUT THE FLESH IS WEAK, AS THEY SAY, AND I'M ONLY--

SCREECH

UNF!

FWAP

YOU SURE ABOUT THAT, OLD MacDONALD?

IT'S A *SECRET* INSTALLATION, YORICK.

IT'S NOT SUPPOSED TO LOOK LIKE THE PENTAGON.

YEAH, BUT A *BARN?*

THAT'S WHERE BANDITS *GO* TO HIDE BEFORE THEY INEVITABLY GET *SHOT* TO DEATH.

JOHN WILKES BOOTH WAS KILLED INSIDE A BARN.

SERIOUSLY, HAVEN'T WE BEEN THROUGH ENOUGH SIEGES ALREADY?

WELL, SEEING AS WE'RE NEITHER OLD-TIMEY OUT-LAWS OR REBEL ASSASSINS, I THINK WE'RE IN THE CLEAR.

AND SINCE WHEN DID *YOU* START ENCOURAGING MAGIC LAD?

SORRY, THREE-FIFTY, BUT I'M STILL FINDING ALL OF THIS A LITTLE HARD TO SWALLOW.

NO, IS *TRUE!* IS EXACTLY AS F.S.B. DESCRIBE TO ME!

FINE, BUT IF THERE ARE ANY *PIGS* IN THERE--

MALE!

48

49

WHOA! EASY, THELMA AND LOUISE!

IT'S JUST DECONTAMINATE.

WE HAVE TO GET THIS MAN TO A STAGING AREA!

NO YOU DON'T. THE KID'S TOTALLY IMMUNE. WE'RE NOT HERE ABOUT HIM.

WHAT THE HELL DO YOU MEAN?

SHE MEANS DON'T PUT AWAY THE E.T. GEAR YET, LADIES.

‡SPTOO‡

YOU'RE ABOUT TO GET SOME OUT-OF-TOWN VISITORS.

YORICK BROWN...

THEY'LL BE LANDING IN YOUR BACKYARD SOON, AND TWO OF THEM ARE *MEN*.

BEFORE LONG, WE'LL HAVE ENOUGH GUYS TO REOPEN THE HE-MAN WOMAN HATER'S CLUB.

Oldenbrook, Kansas
Now

WHAT ARE YOU *TALKING* ABOUT?

OH, IT'S A *LITTLE RASCALS* THING. I DON'T REALLY HATE--

ASTRONAUTS? ARE COMING *HERE*? *HOW*? WHO *ARE* YOU PEOPLE?

I'M AGENT 355. I WORK FOR THE UNITED STATES GOVERNMENT.

THE BOY YOU JUST HOSED DOWN IS YORICK BROWN. WE DON'T KNOW HOW OR WHY HE SURVIVED THE PLAGUE.

BUT WE DO KNOW THAT HE IS A *MAN*, NOT A BOY.

NATALYA ZAMYATIN, SENT BY THE RUSSIANS TO RETRIEVE THEIR COSMONAUT.

DOBRAHYE OOTRAH.

AND AMPERSAND'S TOY OVER THERE IS DR. MANN, A BIOENGINEER OUT OF--

THE DR. MANN?

DR. *ALLISON* MANN?

DID... DID YOU *MAKE* THEM?

THEY'RE NOT CLONES, IDIOT.

THEY'RE *TWINS*.

DOCTOR, MY NAME'S HEATHER HARTLE. THIS IS MY SISTER, HEIDI. WE'RE GENETICISTS.

YOUR JAMA PIECE ON ORGAN BLUEPRINTING MADE ME CRY.

I'M GUESSING YOU'RE NOT SQUATTERS HERE.

NO, WE'RE EMPLOYEES OF THE HOT SUITE.

THE *ONLY* EMPLOYEES. THE REST OF THE STAFF TOOK OFF MONTHS AGO.

YOU MEAN, THERE AREN'T ANY *MEN* ALIVE IN THERE?

NONE OF THE POLITICIANS WHO HAD THIS AS THEIR DESIGNATED *C.O.G.* SITE EVER SHOWED UP. AND ONLY WOMEN EVER WORKED HERE.

MALES HAVE... *TROUBLE* WITH THE ISOLATION.

FUCKING...

FUCK.

I AM SORRY, YORICK, BUT YOUR HOPE IS NOT BEING GONE YET.

IS WHAT HE SAID *TRUE?*

THERE ARE STILL PEOPLE ALIVE ON THE SPACE SHUTTLE?

YOUR GUESS IS AS GOOD AS MINE. I'M JUST GOING ALONG FOR THE RIDE.

LISTEN, WE NEED TO SECURE THIS FACILITY BEFORE THE *SOYUZ* TOUCHES DOWN. IF YOU REFUSE TO LET US INSIDE, MY EXECUTIVE S.C.I. CLEARANCE AUTHORIZES ME TO--

RELAX, LADY. HOUSING PEOPLE IS OUR RAISON D'ETRE. WE'VE BEEN WAITING A *YEAR* FOR SOMETHING LIKE THIS.

YEAH, MI CASA, ETC.

I'D LOVE TO RUN A FEW TESTS ON THE BOY.

JESUS, KILL ME NOW...

58

‹IF WE CAN FIND A WAY TO DO SOMETHING ABOUT HIS CAPTORS.›

‹THIS "CULPER RING" GIRL YORICK'S MOTHER WARNED US ABOUT SEEMS TO HAVE PICKED UP SOME KIND OF MERCENARY, LOOKS LIKE EX-SPETSNAZ.›

‹WAIT, WE'RE GOING TO KIDNAP YORICK FROM HIS KIDNAPPERS?›

‹YOU'RE THE ONE WHO'S SO CONCERNED ABOUT THE "FUTURE OF ISRAEL," NO?›

‹OF COURSE, BUT HOW ARE YOU GOING TO CONVINCE SOME AMERICAN GOY TO REPOPULATE OUR HOMELAND?›

‹PERHAPS WE'LL LOCK HIM IN A ROOM WITH SEVENTY-TWO VIRGINS. I'VE HEARD THAT'S SOME MEN'S IDEA OF HEAVEN.›

‹WHY ARE YOU TALKING ABOUT HIM LIKE HE'S A TERRORIST? HE'S AN INNOCENT BOY!›

‹NONE OF US IS INNOCENT.›

‹OH, SAVE THAT NONSENSE FOR THE NEW GIRLS.›

‹WHAT ARE YOU PLAYING AT HERE? IF WE STEAL YORICK, THE AMERICANS WILL GO TO WAR TO GET HIM BACK.›

‹WE SHOULD BE SO LUCKY.›

⟨WHAT DOES *THAT* MEAN?⟩

⟨YOU SAW WHAT HAPPENED BACK AT THE TEMPLE MOUNT A FEW MONTHS AGO, DIDN'T YOU? BETWEEN OUR OWN PEOPLE? THE RIOTING? THE FISTFIGHTS?⟩

⟨YEAH, WELL, THE ULTRA-ORTHODOX WOMEN INTERPRET THE PLAGUE A LITTLE DIFFERENTLY THAN THE REST OF US. BIG SURPRISE.⟩

⟨WHAT DOES THAT HAVE TO DO WITH *YORICK?*⟩

⟨THE FIGHTING DIDN'T BEGIN IN EARNEST UNTIL THE I.D.F. ... *SEDATED* OUR ARAB NEIGHBORS.⟩

⟨AS SOON AS WE REMOVED ALL OF ISRAEL'S *EXTERNAL* THREATS, THE *INTERNAL* CONFLICT THAT'S BEEN SIMMERING FOR YEARS FINALLY CAME TO A BOIL.⟩

⟨THE SAME THING WILL HAPPEN TO OUR ALLIES IN THE STATES SOON ENOUGH.⟩

⟨WITHOUT AN OUT-SIDE "EVIL" FOR ITS CITIZENS TO HATE, POOR WILL EVENTUALLY TURN AGAINST RICH, WHITE AGAINST BLACK, AND--⟩

⟨WHAT ARE YOU SUGGESTING, THE ONLY WAY TO PROTECT PEACE IN OUR NATIONS IS TO INVENT A *WAR?* WHAT THE HELL KIND OF PLAN IS THAT?⟩

⟨A VERY OLD, VERY *RELIABLE* ONE.⟩

MAN, THIS PLACE IS LIKE *SMALLVILLE* UPSTAIRS, *FORTRESS OF SOLITUDE* DOWNSTAIRS.

YOU CLEAN UP GOOD, YORICK.

COME, ENJOY HOT MUSH IN BAG WITH ME.

OH, GOD, NOT *M.R.E.*s. I LIVED OFF THOSE THINGS FOR A *WEEK* ON MY WAY TO D.C. THE SUPER-MARKETS HAD ALL BEEN RANSACKED, BUT I FOUND SOME DEAD GUY IN PENNSYLVANIA WITH AN OLD *Y2K BUNKER* IN HIS BACKYARD.

FAT LOT OF GOOD PREPARING FOR THE WORST DOES, HUH? EVERY BOY SCOUT THEY TAUGHT TO "BE PREPARED" IS A *CORPSE* NOW.

THANK-FULLY, THAT'S ALSO THE *GIRL* SCOUTS' MOTTO.

I WAS A BROWNIE.

HEATHER AND HEIDI JUST GAVE US A NICKEL TOUR OF THE LOWER LEVEL, AND THEY SEEM *PERFECT.*

THE SPACE CADETS CAN THEORETICALLY SURVIVE DOWN THERE FOR YEARS, UNTIL WE'RE SURE THE PLAGUE'S DISSIPATED.

OR UNTIL DR. MANN COMES UP WITH SOME KIND OF VACCINE.

NO! NOT ACCEPTABLE!

UNITED NATIONS CHARTER SAY, "IF, OWING TO ACCIDENT, DISTRESS, EMERGENCY OR UNINTENDED LANDING, THE PERSONNEL OF A SPACECRAFT LAND IN TERRITORY UNDER THE JURISDICTION OF A CONTRACTING PARTY, THEY SHALL BE SAFELY AND PROMPTLY RETURNED TO REPRESENTATIVES OF THE LAUNCHING AUTHORITY!"

WHAT THE...? *COOKIE MONSTER* SPEAKS BETTER ENGLISH THAN YOU. WHEN THE HELL DID YOU LEARN ALL THAT?

I HAVE LONG BOAT RIDE TO STATES FOR MEMORIZING.

WE HAVE NO INTENTION OF TAKING YOUR MAN *HOSTAGE,* NATALYA. WE'RE JUST HOLDING HIM FOR OBSERVATION.

FOR NOW, I DON'T WANT THE BOYS VENTURING BEYOND THIS SECTOR. YORICK AND AMPERSAND MAY BE IMMUNE TO WHATEVER CAUSED THIS, BUT THERE'S A CHANCE THEY'RE STILL--

BOOOM

WAS THAT...?

SOYUZ.

YOU SAID IT'S NOT SUPPOSED TO BE ENTERING THE ATMOSPHERE FOR ANOTHER *THREE HOURS!*

THEY MUST BE MOVE UP WINDOW TO AVOID STORM OR--

WHATEVER. GRAB YOUR GEAR, NATALYA.

LADIES, YOU'RE AT STANDBY ON THE AIRLOCKS DOWNSTAIRS.

DOCTOR, KEEP AN EYE ON YORICK.

I'D *NEVER* DO ANYTHING TO FUCK THIS UP, 355.

SCOUT'S HONOR.

⟨SHOULD WE BE WORRIED ABOUT THAT SMOKE?⟩

⟨NOT NECESSARILY. THE *R.S.C.* EGGHEADS TOLD ME THE SOFT-LANDING ENGINES MIGHT SINGE PART OF THE FIELD. THE CAPSULE CAN TAKE THE HEAT.⟩

⟨I'M A LITTLE CONCERNED ABOUT THE PLACEMENT, THOUGH. PILOTING THOSE TIN CANS ISN'T AN EXACT SCIENCE, BUT THEY'RE ABOUT THREE VERSTS OUTSIDE THE TARGET ZONE.⟩

⟨VERSTS?⟩

SORRY, IN THE ENGLISH, VERST IS ALMOST ABOUT, EHH... ONE KLICK.

⟨A *KLICK?* THAT'S A REAL WORD? I THOUGHT THEY ONLY USED THAT IN BAD VIETNAM MOVIES.⟩

⟨ARE YOU HIGH? OF COURSE IT'S REAL. A KLICK IS ONE KILOMETER... THAT'S .62 MILES IN *AMERICAN.*⟩

⟨I CAN HANDLE METRIC, SMARTASS. BUT I'VE BEEN PART OF A PARAMILITARY ORGANIZATION SINCE I WAS SIXTEEN, AND I'VE *NEVER* HEARD ANYONE USE--⟩

MOTHERFUCK.

WHO THE FUCK ARE *YOU?*

MOVE AND YOU'RE *DEAD!*

WAIT!

I...I SURRENDER.

JUST DON'T HURT ANYONE ELSE. PLEASE.

YORICK...

TAKE HIM, LADIES. GET THE MONKEY, TOO.

YOU SURE ABOUT THAT?

SHE HAS *AIDS.* AND SHE *BITES.*

AR OH

〈MA'AM?〉

〈FINE, LEAVE THE DAMN ANIMAL WITH THE WOMAN.〉

〈JUST MOVE!〉

‹YOU HEAR THAT? SOUNDS LIKE A *HELICOPTER*... AMERICAN MILITARY?›

‹IS IT COMING OR GOING?›

‹CAN'T TELL.›

‹ALL RIGHT, DON'T SHOOT ANYONE UNTIL WE KNOW THE SCORE.›

‹BUT THOSE ASSHOLES SCAMMED US!›

‹WE DON'T KNOW *WHAT'S* GOING ON, GOD-DAMMIT! JUST KEEP YOUR SAFETY ON UNTIL--›

‹ISRAELIS?›

‹GUN!›

BLAM

69

71

STUPID.

TRISTA... PYATDESYAT...

THREE HUNDRED, IS...IS YOU DEAD?

NATALYA. ARE YOU...?

⟨I'LL ⟩EHN⟨ LIVE. I'M SO SORRY. CAN'T BELIEVE I FUCKING PASSED OUT. LIKE IT'S MY *FIRST* TIME GETTING SHOT. ARE THE OTHERS--⟩

⟨I DON'T KNOW, BUT I THINK THEY GOT YORICK.⟩

⟨A RADIO. ONE OF THEM HAD A *RADIO*...⟩

⟨THERE.⟩

WHOEVER THIS IS, TURN YOUR CRAFT AROUND AND BRING THE MALE BACK *NOW*.

⟩KZACK⟨

AGENT 355, IS IT...?

73

JESUS, MY GAUGES ARE BURIED SO DEEP IN THE RED, SOME OF THEM HAVE GONE *GREEN* AGAIN.

YOU THINK THE WOMEN WILL THROW A PARADE FOR US, VLAD?

I SHOULD HOPE SO, SIR. ONE TO RIVAL GAGARIN'S IN '61.

I KNOW WHY YOU BOYS ARE JOKING, BUT I'M TELLING YOU THAT YOU *SHOULD* BE STRESSED. IF WE CAN'T KEEP SHOCK NEUTRALIZATION ONLINE--

WHO DO YOU THINK THEY'LL HAVE WAITING FOR US DOWN THERE, VLAD? SOME OF THOSE SEXY NURSES?

PERHAPS A FEW OF YOUR CHEERLEADERS.

Oldenbrook, Kansas
Now

SHUT THE HELL UP, NATALYA!

〈WHAT RIGHT DO YOU HAVE TO SURRENDER *MY* MAN? I TRAVELED ACROSS A GODDAMN OCEAN TO RETURN OUR ONE FUCKING COSMONAUT TO--〉

IF YOU DON'T SHUT YOUR MOUTH, YOU'RE GOING TO HAVE A *SECOND* BULLET IN YOU. AND I GUARANTEE I'M A BETTER SHOT THAN *THEY* WERE.

IS EVERYTHING ALL RIGHT, AGENT?

LISTEN CAREFULLY, MY TEAM AND I ARE GOING TO PICK UP THE MEN AT THEIR EMERGENCY LANDING ZONE AND BRING THEM BACK TO THE FACILITY WHERE YOU STOLE YORICK.

YOU'LL MEET US THERE LATER TONIGHT, AND WE'LL MAKE THE TRADE.

YOU ASSUME THAT I THINK YOUR STORY IS *TRUE.*

BESIDES, EVEN IF IT *WERE,* WHY WOULD YOU SACRIFICE TWO GROWN MEN FOR ONE SCRAWNY BOY?

HEY! ASSHOLE! THIS BAG ISN'T SOUNDPROOF!

BECAUSE, I'M... I'M IN LOVE WITH HIM.

SHE'S WHAT?

WELL... THIS IS FINALLY STARTING TO MAKE SENSE.

FINE THEN, WE WILL MEET YOU TONIGHT. BUT IF YOUR SPACESHIP FAILS TO APPEAR...YOU WILL NEVER SEE YOUR BOYFRIEND AGAIN.

ALTER OUT.

‹PILOT, SET US DOWN!›

‹WE HAVE WORK TO DO...›

‹YOU DESPERATE FUCKING IDIOT. THEY'LL *NEVER* GIVE YOU YORICK BACK!›

‹THEY'RE GOING TO TAKE MY COUNTRY'S ONLY MAN FOR THEMSELVES AND *SLAUGHTER* THE REST OF US! AND FOR WHAT, SOME STUPID *CRUSH?*›

DON'T BE DENSE, NATALYA. I'M NOT LETTING THEM TAKE YOUR COSMONAUT, AND I'M *DEFINITELY* NOT IN LOVE WITH YORICK.

I ONLY SAID THAT TO GET THEM BACK HERE.

‹SORRY, MY ENGLISH MUST *BLOW*...I THOUGHT YOU JUST SAID THAT YOU'RE DELIBERATELY LURING AN ENTIRE *PLATOON* BACK TO THE PEOPLE WHO *KILLED* TWO OF THEIR SOLDIERS!›

355!

DR. MANN!

THEY... THEY GOT YORICK.

I KNOW. IS EVERYONE OKAY?

I'LL LIVE, BUT THOSE THUGS TOSSED HEATHER AND HEIDI A PRETTY GOOD BEATING ON THEIR WAY INSIDE THE COMPOUND.

DID...DID WE JUST GET RAIDED BY *ISRAELIS?*

WHY? I MEAN, WE'RE *JEWISH!*

WE'LL WORRY ABOUT MOTIVES LATER. RIGHT NOW, I NEED YOU TO FIX NATALYA'S SHOULDER AS BEST YOU CAN.

WE HAVE WORK TO DO...

IT'S A TRAP!

SHE...SHE MADE UP THAT BULLSHIT ABOUT NASA DUDES TO TRICK YOU. LET'S JUST GET OUT OF HERE AND PROCEED WITH THE TORTURING OR WHATEVER.

⟨THE MORE HE OBJECTS, THE MORE I BELIEVE THE AMERICAN GIRL'S ASSERTION.⟩

⟨I'M NOT SURE, ALTER. IT STILL SOUNDS PREPOSTEROUS TO ME.⟩

⟨EITHER WAY, A BOY IN THE HAND IS WORTH TWO IN THE BUSH, NO?⟩

⟨SADIE, IF ANY- ONE OTHER THAN ISRAEL ACQUIRES MALES, OUR NATION LOSES THE LEVERAGE AND POSITION THAT COME WITH HAVING YORICK.⟩

⟨SO WHAT, YOU'RE GOING TO HOLD ON TO THE BOY AND MAKE A PLAY FOR THE ASTRONAUTS?⟩

⟨I'M DOING WHAT I HAVE TO DO.⟩

⟨BUT YORICK'S PROBABLY RIGHT ABOUT THE AMERICANS SETTING A TRAP INSIDE THAT BARN!⟩

⟨THAT'S WHY WE'RE TAKING THE FIGHT OUTSIDE.⟩

⟨NAIM, I WANT YOU TO LEAD THE REST OF THE UNIT BACK TOWARDS THE FACILITY WE STORMED. FROM A SAFE DISTANCE, SHADOW THE AMERICANS TO THE LANDING ZONE.⟩

⟨THE CULPER RING AGENT HAS ONE OF OUR HANDHELDS, SO MAINTAIN RADIO SILENCE UNTIL I CONTACT YOU WITH FURTHER INSTRUCTIONS.⟩

BEHATZLACHA!

⟨I SHOULD GO WITH THEM, ALTER. THOSE GIRLS ARE BARELY FIELD RATED, AND NAIM ISN'T EXACTLY **LEADERSHIP MATERIAL.**⟩

⟨I WANT YOU WITH ME, SADIE.⟩

⟨IF THIS 355 IS SMART, SHE'S ALREADY DISPATCHED PART OF HER TEAM TO LOOK FOR YORICK. IT WILL TAKE US BOTH TO GUARD HIM.⟩

UM, I MAY NOT SPEAK HEBREW, BUT IT'S PRETTY CLEAR WHEN YOU'RE TALKING ABOUT **ME.** ALL I HEAR IS, "GIBBERISH GIBBERISH **YORICK** GIBBERISH."

YOU'RE A HEARTBEAT AWAY FROM BEING GAGGED, MR. BROWN.

AND I THINK THAT I'M STARTING TO UNDERSTAND THIS BLACK SACK ROUTINE, TOO.

IT'S NOT ABOUT KEEPING ME IN THE DARK, RIGHT? IT'S ABOUT HELPING YOU PRETEND THAT I'M JUST AN **OBJECT** AND NOT A--

IF I REMOVE IT, WILL YOU PROMISE TO STOP BLABBERING?

OW. PUPILS... **CONSTRICTING.**

⟨SADIE, KEEP A CLOSE EYE ON OUR GUEST.⟩

APPARENTLY, HE FANCIES HIMSELF QUITE THE ESCAPE ARTIST.

OOO, AM I SUPPOSED TO BE IMPRESSED BY YOUR SCARY "INTEL"?

EVERYONE WHO'S READ MY AWARD-WINNING *NEWSLETTER* KNOWS WHAT I DO.

NO, YOU'RE SUPPOSED TO BE IMPRESSED BY THE *HANDCUFFS* YOU'VE BEEN TRYING TO FREE YOURSELF FROM FOR THE LAST HOUR.

THEY WERE DESIGNED BY MOSSAD TO BE ONE HUNDRED PERCENT UNPICKABLE.

THE ONLY PALESTINIAN EVER TO BREAK OUT OF MEGIDDO PRISON STILL HAD TO SAW OFF HIS LEFT HAND TO GET OUT OF--

ARE YOU TAUNTING ME WITH A MANIACAL *DEATHTRAP?* WHAT ARE YOU, A *BATMAN* VILLAIN?

SERIOUSLY, I THOUGHT YOU PEOPLE WERE SUPPOSED TO BE THE *GOOD GUYS.*

NO MATTER WHAT STUPID SHIT YOUR PRIME MINISTER EVER DID, MY PARENTS WERE ALWAYS HUGE SUPPORTERS OF ISRAEL. I MEAN, DO YOU EVEN KNOW WHO MY *MOTHER* IS?

⟨BETTER THAN YOU DO, I SUSPECT.⟩

WHAT DID YOU JUST SAY? DID YOU JUST INSULT MY *MOM?* SAY IT IN ENGLISH, G.I. JANE, I *DARE* YOU!

⟨CUFF HIM TO ONE OF THE CHAIRS INSIDE THE COPTER.⟩

⟨IF HE REFUSES TO BE SILENT, KNOCK HIM *UNCONSCIOUS.*⟩

84

YOU SURE WE'RE IN THE RIGHT PLACE?

POSITIVE. ALL WE HAVE TO DO NOW IS WAIT.

I STILL DON'T UNDERSTAND WHY *I* HAD TO COME ALONG, 355.

I TOLD YOU, WE NEED THE TWINS ON CALL BACK AT THE HOT SUITE.

--IS DOING WHAT *I* **ASKED** HER TO DO, DOCTOR. IF MY PLAN WORKS, WE'LL BE ABLE TO HOLD ON TO THE ASTRONAUTS **AND** GET YORICK BACK.

BUT NATALYA--

AND IF IT DOESN'T?

⟨IS THAT HER, NAIM? IS SHE THE ONE WHO KILLED SELTZER AND KLARSFELD?⟩

⟨HOW THE HELL AM I SUPPOSED TO KNOW? BESIDES, WE'RE NOT HERE TO GET REVENGE.⟩

⟨NOT **YET**, ANYWAY...⟩

HEY, YOU SPEAK ENGLISH?

BE QUIET.

I'LL TAKE THAT AS A *YES*. LISTEN, YOU'RE OBVIOUSLY NOT CRAZY ABOUT THIS WHOLE CAMPAIGN. IT'S WRITTEN ALL OVER YOUR FACE.

IF YOU ARE TRYING TO WIN MY FAVOR, I WOULD ADVISE YOU AGAINST COMPARING ME TO PEOPLE WHO KILLED MY *GREAT GRAND-FATHER*.

MAYBE YOU THINK YOU'RE JUST FOLLOWING ORDERS HERE...BUT DON'T FORGET HOW THAT EXCUSE WENT OVER AT *NUREMBERG*.

OH.

BESIDES, THAT WOMAN TOOK A *BULLET* FOR ME IN HEBRON. HOW...HOW COULD I JUST BETRAY HER *NOW*? HOW COULD I--

SADIE!

GET OUT HERE. SOMETHING'S HAPPENING.

88

‹WE DON'T HAVE TIME TO BE PRECIOUS ABOUT THIS, SADIE. WE ONLY NEED ONE MAN TO ENSURE OUR NATION'S SECURITY. OTHERS WOULD JUST BECOME LIABILITIES.›

‹I ASKED YOU TO STAY WITH ME BECAUSE I KNOW YOU'RE--›

‹PUT IT DOWN.›

‹...INTERESTING.›

‹I PRESUME YOU STILL REMEMBER THE PUNISHMENT FOR *TREASON*?›

‹THIS HAS TO STOP, ALTER. I'M BEGINNING TO REALIZE THAT A NEVER-ENDING BATTLE IS JUST A...A WAR WITHOUT *WINNERS.*›

‹YOU'RE MAKING A VERY BAD DECISION.›

‹MAYBE, BUT AT LEAST I'M FINALLY MAKING ONE. THAT'S SOMETHING I SHOULD HAVE DONE A LONG TIME--›

HOLY **SHIT!**

WHAT **WAS** THAT?

≷KOFF≷
≷KOFF≷
≷KOFF≷

YOU FUCKING **ANIMAL!**

IF THAT MISSILE HAD HIT THOSE PEOPLE, I'D HAVE CHOKED THE LIFE RIGHT OUT OF YOUR GODDAMN--

‹NAIM... DON'T LET THEM...GET TO THE SPACE-CRAFT...›

WHAT ARE YOU DOING?

STOP IT!

‹...TERMINATE...THE **AMERICANS...**›

POOR DUMB KIDS.

LIKE HITTING FISHES IN BUCKET...

LISTEN UP! I'M SURE AT LEAST ONE OF YOU SPEAKS ENGLISH, SO SPREAD THE WORD!

AT THE COUNT OF THREE, I AM GOING TO STAND BACK UP. IF YOU HAVE ALL DROPPED YOUR WEAPONS AND PUT YOUR HANDS IN THE AIR, NO ONE ELSE WILL BE HARMED.

THIS IS NEVER GOING TO WORK, 355! THERE ARE LIKE A DOZEN OF THEM AND ONLY TWO OF--

IF YOU TRY TO KILL ME, YOU MIGHT SUCCEED, BUT MY SNIPER WILL STOP AIMING FOR APPENDAGES AND START HITTING *FACES.* THE CHOICE IS YOURS!

ONE... *TWO...*

THREE.

WOW.

COLLECT THEIR WEAPONS AND PUT THEM INTO ZIP TIES, DOCTOR. NATALYA HAS YOUR BACK, SO DON'T BE SCARED.

ISRAELI COMMAND, THIS IS AGENT 355. YOUR GREED JUST *INVALIDATED* OUR DEAL.

I'M CURRENTLY HOLDING YOUR ENTIRE REGIMENT HOSTAGE, AND WON'T RETURN THEM UNTIL I HAVE OUR MAN BACK.

THAT WAS YOUR MASTER PLAN, JOAN OF ARC? YOU REALLY THINK THIS LUNATIC WOULD HAVE TRADED *MOI* FOR A FEW WORTHLESS *GIRL GRUNTS?*

YORICK?

YOU *ESCAPED?*

WELL, THAT'S A RELATIVE TERM.

BUT FORGET ABOUT ME, WHAT'S THE WORD ON MAJOR TOM AND FRIENDS?

I'M NOT SURE YET. I KNEW THE ISRAELIS WOULD TRAIL US, SO WE LED THEM TO A *FAKE* LANDING ZONE. I'M HEADED FOR THE REAL ONE NOW.

I SEE SMOKE, BUT NATALYA SAID TO EXPECT THAT.

THING DID LOOK LIKE IT WAS COMING IN PRETTY FAST THOUGH, DIDN'T IT?

OKAY, I'M COMING UP ON IT AND--

{HZZZ} {KZACK} EEEEEE

THAT'S NOT FUNNY, 355!

COME ON, KNOCK OFF THE "TO BE CONTINUED" SHIT! WHAT'S GOING ON?

HELLO?

Oldenbrook, Kansas
Now

355!

DR. MANN?!

YOU'RE SUPPOSED TO BE GUARDING THE--

NATALYA'S GOT THE ISRAELIS UNDER CONTROL. SHE TOLD ME TO GIVE YOU A HAND WITH--

THEY'RE ALIVE!

WE *HAVE* TO HELP THEM!

NO!

BUT THEY'VE BEEN IN ZERO GRAVITY FOR *MONTHS!* THEY CAN'T WALK WITHOUT--

I'LL TAKE CARE OF IT, DOCTOR!

YOU JUST STAY THE HELL BACK!

ARE YOU ALL RIGHT?

HYDRAZINE LEAK... IN THE CABIN...

STAY CALM! {KOFF}

I'M GOING TO {KOFF} {KOFF} {KOFF}

COME ON! WE *NEED* TO GET THEM OUT OF HERE!

DOCTOR, I TOLD YOU--

UHF!

SHUT THE FUCK UP AND CARRY!

SLOW DOWN! WE CAN'T RISK TEARING THEIR SUITS! IF WHATEVER KILLED ALL THE MEN IS STILL IN THE ATMOSPHERE, IT COULD--

THEY SAID THERE'S A *HYDRAZINE LEAK*, GODDAMMIT! IF WE DON'T HURRY, THE WHOLE SOYUZ COULD--

102

WHAT DOES *THAT* MEAN?

IT MEANS ONLY THE *FEMALE* SURVIVED.

I'M SO SORRY.

GET AWAY FROM ME!

THE ACCIDENT. IT WASN'T CAUSED BY *ALTER*... WAS IT?

WHAT DO YOU CARE, *ASSHOLE?*

SADIE. MY NAME IS SADIE.

AND WHY DO YOU THINK I WAS KNOCKED OUT? I TRIED TO *STOP* HER. I--

DON'T!

I KICKED THE SHIT OUT OF YOUR BOSS AND I... I CAN DO THE SAME TO YOU.

IT'S NOT A WEAPON, YORICK.

IT'S A TRUCE.

IF THIS IS SOME KIND OF CHEAP *PLOY...*

NO. NO MORE GAMES. I'M TIRED OF PLAYING ARMY.

GO, HELP YOUR FRIENDS.

THEY *ARE* FRIENDS, RIGHT? NOT CAPTORS?

CAPTORS? OF COURSE NOT. WHO TOLD YOU...

IT DOESN'T MATTER. OUR INTELLIGENCE WAS POOR FOR THIS MISSION. NOT THAT IT EXCUSES OUR *ACTIONS...*

I PROMISE TO WAIT HERE WITH ALTER UNTIL YOUR PEOPLE DECIDE WHAT PUNISHMENT THE TWO OF US DESERVE.

I ONLY ASK THAT YOU SHOW MERCY TO THE OTHER GIRLS. THEY'RE NOT TO BLAME FOR OUR--

OH, SAVE THE *A FEW GOOD MEN* CRAP. ALL OF THE GOOD MEN ARE *DEAD.*

JUST TELL ME...WHY DID YOU PEOPLE DO THIS? AMERICA AND ISRAEL ARE SUPPOSED TO BE *FRIENDS.*

DON'T YOU KNOW? THIS IS WHAT HAPPENS TO FRIENDS WHEN A *MAN* COMES BETWEEN THEM.

ANYBODY HOME...?

AK AK AK

AHH!

OH...HEY, AMPERSAND.

NICE TO SEE YOU, TOO, BUDDY.

BUT WHAT IS THAT *SMELL* ON YOUR HANDS?

YORICK!

355.

YOU OKAY?

NOT EVEN CLOSE.

HOW'S OUR SPACE CADET?

RECOVERING DOWN IN THE HOT SUITE. DR. MANN AND THE TWINS THINK SHE'S GONNA BE FINE.

BUT YORICK, THE TWO MEN...

I KNOW, I HEARD. NATALYA FILLED ME IN ON THE WHOLE NIGHTMARE WHILE WE TOOK CARE OF THOSE ISRAELI SOLDIERS YOU CAPTURED.

WAIT, TOOK CARE OF THEM HOW?

WE MARCHED THEM BACK TO SADIE. SHE'S A TRAINED MEDIC, SO SHE CAN PATCH UP THE GIRLS YOU GUYS PUT HOLES IN.

WHO THE HELL IS *SADIE*?

THEIR NEW LEADER. THE OLD ONE'S BEEN HOGTIED AND COURT-MARTIALED OR WHATEVER, SO SADIE'S IN CHARGE NOW. SHE'S GOOD PEOPLE.

SHE HELPED *KIDNAP* YOU!

YEAH, AND THEN SHE HELPED ME ESCAPE.

SO WHAT, NOW WE'RE JUST SUPPOSED TO *LET THEM GO*?

WHAT CHOICE DO WE HAVE, 355? ARE WE GONNA BUILD A P.O.W. CAMP FOR THE WHOLE PLATOON?

BESIDES, NATALYA'S DESTROYING ALL OF THEIR WEAPONS AS WE SPEAK. THEY'RE BEATEN AND BROKEN, AND...AND ALL THEY CAN DO NOW IS HEAD BACK TO ISRAEL WITH THEIR TAILS BETWEEN THEIR LEGS, RIGHT?

THAT'S A PRETTY MAGNANIMOUS GESTURE COMING FROM THE GUY WHO WANTED TO LOCK UP EVERY WOMAN IN SIGHT BACK IN MARRISVILLE.

YEAH, I... I KNOW.

BUT IT WAS EITHER THAT OR LINE THEM UP IN FRONT OF A FIRING SQUAD.

AND I'VE HAD JUST ABOUT ALL THE DEATH I CAN TAKE FOR A WHILE.

BUT YORICK, THAT THING THAT ALMOST HIT THE SOYUZ...

DON'T WORRY, THAT WAS *ALTER*, NOT SADIE.

I TRIED TO STOP HER FROM FIRING IT, BUT I GUESS I ONLY MANAGED TO KNOCK THE MISSILE OFF COURSE.

HOLD ON, YOU TOOK DOWN A SOLDIER ARMED WITH A *ROCKET LAUNCHER*?

I KNOW, I'M SORRY. I SWEAR, I *TRY* TO STAY OUT OF TROUBLE, BUT--

YOU DON'T NEED TO *APOLOGIZE*, 'RICK. YOU SAVED A WOMAN'S *LIFE*.

WELL, THAT PRETTY MUCH DEFINES A *PYRRHIC* VICTORY, DOESN'T IT?

I MEAN, THE LAST TWO MEN WHO ACTUALLY HAD SOMETHING TO OFFER THE WORLD ARE *GONE*. NOW THE FATE OF HUMANITY IS BACK ON *MY* WORTHLESS SHOULDERS.

OH, KNOCK OFF THE SELF-DEPRECATING BULLSHIT.

I'M NOT SAYING I WANT YOU TO KEEP PULLING YOUR STUPID STUNTS, BUT YOU DID OKAY TODAY. YOU'RE A *HERO*.

CHRIST, PLEASE DON'T USE THAT WORD. IF THERE'S ONE THING I NEVER WANT TO BECOME...

OH, GOD.

YOUR *SISTER*. I DIDN'T MEAN...

DANGER!
BIOSAFETY LEVEL 4
AIR-LOCK DOOR/DECON SHOWER
NO ENTRY WITHOUT HAZMAT SUIT

DR. WEBER?

GOD, NO ONE'S CALLED ME THAT IN **MONTHS.**

CIBA IS FINE.

CIBA, I'M DR. MANN. I HELPED BRING YOU IN. MY CONDOLENCES ABOUT THE...THE...

EXCUSE ME?

THE L.O.C.V.

"LOSS OF CREW AND VEHICLE."

NASA NEVER MET A CATASTROPHE IT COULDN'T DISTILL INTO AN ACRONYM.

MY CREW-MATES. WERE YOU ABLE TO RECOVER ANY...ANY REMAINS?

NOT YET. THE TEMPERATURE OF THE BLAST...

IF IT'S ANY CONSOLATION, THEY DIED INSTANTLY.

NO OFFENSE, DOCTOR, BUT I DON'T THINK THAT PHRASE HAS EVER BEEN ANY CONSOLATION TO ANYONE.

CIBA, WHAT...WHAT *HAPPENED?*

EXPIRED CHEMICALS INSIDE THE SOYUZ CORRODED PART OF OUR BOAT'S INTERIOR. WE MADE IT THROUGH REENTRY OKAY, BUT ALL HELL BROKE LOOSE WHEN WE FIRED THE SOFT-LANDING ENGINES.

I REALIZE THAT, BUT...

FORGIVE ME IF THIS IS INDELICATE, BUT YOU THREE HAD RADIO CONTACT WITH THE RUSSIANS. YOU *KNEW* ABOUT THE PLAGUE, YOU KNEW ALL OF THE MEN WERE *DEAD* DOWN HERE...

...SO WHY DID THE TWO PRECIOUS MALES ON BOARD LET A USELESS *WOMAN* ESCAPE FIRST?

I'M SORRY.

NO, BELIEVE ME, I SCREAMED THE SAME THING, BUT THE BOYS WOULDN'T LISTEN.

AS SOON AS WE BLEW THE EXPLOSIVE BOLTS ON THE HATCH, JOE AND VLAD STARTED PUSHING ME OUTSIDE. THEY KEPT SAYING THE SAME THING OVER AND OVER...

"WOMEN AND CHILDREN FIRST."

THEY JEOPARDIZED THE FUTURE OF MANKIND...FOR *CHIVALRY?*

NEVER. THOSE TWO MEN WERE THE BRAVEST, MOST NOBLE...

DOCTOR, WHEN THEY SAID "WOMEN AND CHILDREN," THEY MEANT IT *LITERALLY.*

YOU MEAN, YOU'RE...YOU'RE *PREGNANT?*

YOU HAVE TO UNDER-STAND, WE WERE UP THERE FOR ALMOST A *YEAR.* WE WERE SCARED AND LONELY AND...AND NONE OF US REALLY THOUGHT WE WOULD MAKE IT BACK ALIVE.

JESUS, WHICH ONE IS THE *FATHER?*

I LOVED THEM BOTH SO MUCH.

SO FUCKING MUCH...

I DON'T KNOW.

115

A *BABY?*

DO WE KNOW THE SEX YET?

SHE'S ONLY THREE WEEKS ALONG, TOO EARLY TO TELL.

BUT IF HER CHILD *IS* MALE, IT SHOULD BE FINE.

YOU BROUGHT THE MOTHER INSIDE IN AN UNCOMPROMISED SUIT, SO THEY THEORETICALLY HAVEN'T BEEN EXPOSED TO ANY POSSIBLE REMNANTS OF THE PLAGUE.

AND WE HAVE MORE THAN ENOUGH SUPPLIES FOR CIBA TO SPEND THE DURATION OF HER PREGNANCY IN A CLEAN ENVIRONMENT.

CLEAN, MAYBE, BUT NOT *SECURE*...IF THE ISRAELIS WERE ABLE TO FIND THIS PLACE, SO CAN OTHERS.

YEAH, BUT WE CAN'T EXACTLY BRING A PREGNANT LADY IN A SPACESUIT WITH US TO CALIFORNIA, CAN WE? THAT WOULD MAKE FOR A GREAT SITCOM, BUT A LOUSY ROAD TRIP.

WE CAN'T JUST LEAVE THESE PEOPLE ALONE AND DEFENSELESS, YORICK.

NO, YOU CANNOT...

...THIS IS WHY YOU WILL PLEASE BE LEAVING THEM IN THE COMPANY OF *ME*.

BECAUSE OF ISRAEL WOMENS, I NOW HAVE MANY OF BANGING ARTILLERY TO USE ON ANYONE WHO MIGHT BROUGHT TROUBLE IN.

MAN, I WOULD *LOVE* TO DIAGRAM THAT SENTENCE.

〈NATALYA, WE CAN'T ASK YOU TO STAY. YOU'VE DONE SO MUCH ALREADY. YOU DESERVE TO GO *HOME*.〉

〈I APPRECIATE THE OFFER, PAL, BUT I CAN'T GO BACK TO RUSSIA, NOT EMPTY-HANDED.〉

〈BESIDES, I DEDICATED MY *LIFE* TO RETRIEVING OUR LAST MAN. NOW THAT HE'S PASSED, I'M A SHIP WITHOUT A RUDDER. LOOKING AFTER THIS KID MIGHT STOP ME FROM, YOU KNOW, *CAPSIZING*.〉

WHAT ABOUT ME? SOMEONE WILL HAVE TO RUN TESTS AND COLLECT GENETIC SAMPLES AND--

MY SISTER AND I ARE MORE THAN QUALIFIED TO HANDLE THAT, DR. MANN. YOU SHOULD PRESS ON TO YOUR BACKUP LAB, CONTINUE YOUR RESEARCH ON YORICK AND HIS PET.

WHAT'S THE HURRY? WE CAN STICK AROUND LONG ENOUGH TO PASS OUT CIGARS AND SHIT, CAN'T WE? THERE MIGHT BE A BOUNCING BABY *BOY* ON THE WAY!

IF THE FETUS **IS** MALE, WE CAN'T KEEP ALL OF OUR EGGS IN ONE BASKET...OR SPERM IN ONE BARN, AS THE CASE MAY BE.

WE HAVE TO GET YORICK OUT OF HERE **ASAP.**

SORRY, LADIES, I GUESS THAT'S OUR CUE. WE LIKE TO STORM INTO TOWN, INFLICT MAXIMUM DAMAGE, AND THEN DISAPPEAR...LIKE A **KISS** CONCERT.

ONLY WITH LESS UNINTENDED PREGNANCIES IN OUR WAKE.

HEY, IT WAS NICE OF YOU TO BRING A LITTLE EXCITEMENT OUR WAY, DOCTOR.

DOSVIDANYA, ZAMYATIN. I WISH I COULD HAVE HEARD THE STORY BEHIND THAT GOLD STAR OF YOURS.

⟨AND PERHAPS YOU STILL WILL.⟩

⟨UNTIL THEN, KEEP YOUR POWDER DRY AND ALL THAT.⟩

LATER, NATALYA. THANKS FOR, WELL, "HOPE" IS A CORNY WORD, BUT--

YOU ARE GOOD BOY, YORICK.

WHEN YOU ARE DONE, YOU MAY EVEN BE OKAY **MAN.**

⟨I'M SORRY ABOUT THIS, ALTER, BUT IT DOES MAKE THINGS EASIER.⟩

⟨TELL ME, SADIE, HOW DO YOU THINK THE LEGION OF WOMEN STILL LOYAL TO ME IN ISRAEL WILL HANDLE YOUR LITTLE *COUP?*⟩

⟨I SUPPOSE WE'LL CROSS THAT BRIDGE WHEN WE MAKE IT BACK HOME...*IF* WE MAKE IT. WE STILL HAVE TO REPAIR THE TROOP TRANSPORT AND--⟩

⟨COLONEL, SECURE FREQUENCY FOR YOU.⟩

⟨WHAT DID WE DISCUSS, NAIM? NO MORE RANKS.⟩

⟨SORRY, UM, *SADIE.*⟩

⟨IT'S THE AMERICAN POLITICIAN.⟩

⟨NO, WE'RE DONE BEING MANIPULATED BY WOMEN WHOSE POWER HAS MADE THEM *PARANOID.*⟩

⟨SO WHAT SHOULD I DO?⟩

⟨TELL HER WE HAVE ONLY ONE THING TO SAY TO HER...⟩

119

Washington, D.C.
Now

Comedy & Tragedy

Act One of Two: "Comedy"

ALL IS READY, FREDERIC, YOUR CREW AWAITS YOU!

WHAT THE...?

GOD-DAMMIT, MANDA!

YOU'RE NOT SUPPOSED TO ENTER UNTIL *AFTER* THE SONG!

HUH? OH, SORRY, EDIE. THIS...THIS IS MY FIRST PLAY, 'MEMBER?

WEREN'T BOTH OF YOUR FATHERS *GAY?*

YOU SHOULD HAVE A FUCKING *GENETIC PREDISPOSITION* FOR MUSICAL THEATER.

DON'T TALK ABOUT MY DADS!

HO HO, YOU REALLY WANNA TAKE ON EIGHT CREDITS OF STAGE COMBAT FROM STELLA ADLER?

TASTE IRON, SHORTIE!

KNOCK IT OFF, GIRLS!

127

SAVE THE CATTY SHIT FOR BROADWAY, EDIE.

THE REST OF YOU, LET'S TAKE FIVE!

SORRY, CAYCE, BUT IF WE'RE GONNA KEEP PICKING UP LITTLE ORPHAN ANNIES IN EVERY TOWN WE HIT, IT WOULD BE NICE IF ONE OF THEM COULD ACTUALLY *ACT* LIKE ANNIE.

GROW UP, EDIE.

YOU'RE JUST JEALOUS BECAUSE MANDA'S VOCAL RANGE SPANS MORE THAN *ONE OCTAVE*.

CAYCE, LUV, ARE YOU SURE ABOUT THIS FENCING BUSINESS? IT'S NOT IN THE SCRIPT, AND IT DOES STRIKE ME AS BEING RATHER... *GRATUITOUS*.

BESIDES, IT'S NOT AS IF THERE WILL EVER BE ANY *MALES* IN OUR AUDIENCE. WOMEN ARE MORE INTERESTED IN DRAMA AND ROMANCE THAN PUNCHING AND KICKING.

YOU CAN'T MAKE GENERALIZATIONS LIKE THAT, HENRIETTA! NOW THAT ALL OF THE MEN ARE GONE, WE HAVE TO START *EXPLODING* MYTHS ABOUT GENDER AND--

UM... EXCUSE ME?

ARE YOU PEOPLE THE PLAY ACTORS?

I...I WAS GIVEN A *FLYER*.

YES, MA'AM. WE'RE THE HUMBLE MEMBERS OF THE FISH & BICYCLE TRAVELING THEATER TROUPE. I'M OUR DIRECTOR AND SOMETIMES PLAYWRIGHT, CAYCE THOMAS.

YOU MUST BE THE MAYOR OF...FORGIVE ME, WHERE THE HELL ARE WE AGAIN?

NORTHLAKE. *NEBRASKA*. AND I WOULDN'T EXACTLY CALL MYSELF A MAYOR... MORE LIKE A *DEN MOTHER*. HEH.

SO, YOU FOLKS PUT ON SHOWS AND WHATNOT?

WE TRY OUR BEST. MY COMPANIONS AND I REPRESENT A CONFEDERATION OF CREATORS AND PERFORMERS WHO BANDED TOGETHER AFTER THE PLAGUE STRUCK.

WITH THE LACK OF DEPENDABLE ELECTRICITY THROUGHOUT THE COUNTRY, WE REALIZE THAT MOVIES, TELEVISION AND EVEN RADIO ARE LARGELY UNAVAILABLE, SO WE BRING OUR LO-TECH BRAND OF ART FROM TOWN TO TOWN AND--

DO YOU TAKE REQUESTS?

AH... **WHAT?**

YOU SEE, A LOT OF THE GIRLS AND I WERE FANS OF A PROGRAM CALLED AS THE WORLD TURNS.

I KNOW IT MIGHT SOUND SILLY, BUT WE WERE HOPING THAT YOU COULD PICK UP WHERE SOME OF THE STORYLINES LEFT OFF AND--

THAT'S...NOT REALLY WHAT WE DO, MA'AM.

ARE YOU SURE?

BECAUSE I BROUGHT SIX MONTHS' WORTH OF THE SOAP OPERA DIGEST.

IF YOU COULD JUST ACT OUT WHAT HAPPENED TO LLOYD THE BARTENDER AND THAT PRETTY KATE GIRL--

WOULDN'T YOU RATHER SEE SOMETHING A BIT MORE...ARTISTIC?

HOW ABOUT PIRATES OF PENZANCE?

IT'S A KICK-ASS GILBERT & SULLIVAN MUSICAL, A SATIRE ABOUT A SHELTERED YOUNG MAN WHO GETS SWEPT UP IN AN ADVENTURE WITH--

THE ONLY MUSICAL I'VE EVER SEEN IS THAT MOULIN ROUGE.

I...DIDN'T REALLY CARE FOR IT.

WELL, WE, UH, ALSO HAVE A VERY THOUGHT-PROVOKING ALL-FEMALE PRODUCTION OF MAMET'S GLENGARRY GLEN ROSS.

THAT WOULDN'T HAVE ANY SWEARS IN IT, WOULD IT?

ACTUALLY, HOW ABOUT IF WE GO AHEAD AND PICK A PLAY *FOR* YOU? I PROMISE WE'LL FIND A PERFECT FIT.

IF YOU SAY SO.

AS FOR THE COST...?

NOT TO WORRY, WE'RE A STRICTLY NON-PROFIT ORGANIZATION. ALL WE ASK IS A DONATION OF ONE CANNED FOOD ITEM PER AUDIENCE MEMBER.

AND PREFERABLY SOMETHING OTHER THAN *CUTTLEFISH,* PLEASE.

WE GOT STUCK WITH EIGHTY CANS OF THAT BARF DURING A RUN OF *ARCADIA* IN CHEYENNE.

OH, THAT SHOULDN'T BE A PROBLEM.

NORTHLAKE IS THE CANNING FACTORY CAPITAL OF NEBRASKA. WE HAVE ENOUGH FOOD TO LAST US UNTIL KINGDOM COME.

WHAT WE *DON'T* HAVE IS ENTERTAINMENT.

OUR LIBRARY'S BEEN PRETTY WELL PILLAGED, AND THE GIRLS COULD SURE USE A BIT OF AN ESCAPE.

OF COURSE, I... I UNDERSTAND.

THERE'S A SMALL PLAYHOUSE IN TOWN SQUARE. IT'S NOT MUCH, BUT WE SHOULD HAVE ENOUGH GAS TO POWER THE FOOTLIGHTS FOR A FEW NIGHTS. AS FOR ACCOMMODATIONS, I'M AFRAID WE'RE SHORT ON--

WE'RE MORE THAN HAPPY TO SLEEP UNDER THE STARS, MA'AM.

FOR NOW, LET'S SAY THAT WE'LL DEBUT THIS FRIDAY EVENING, AND PLAN FOR AN ENCORE ON SATURDAY, MAYBE A SUNDAY MATINEE IN CASE OF OVERFLOW.

MARVELOUS! GOD BLESS YOU GOOD PEOPLE FOR YOUR SERVICE! I'LL HAVE SOME OF MY HOMEMADE HOTCAKES WAITING AT THE PLAYHOUSE TOMORROW MORNING!

EXPLODING MYTHS ABOUT GENDER, EH?

YEAH... KA-BOOM.

TROUBLE SLEEPING, FEARLESS LEADER?

HEY, HENRIETTA. I WAS JUST TRYING TO FIND A WAY TO MAKE OUR PENZANCE PRODUCTION MORE, I DON'T KNOW...*RELEVANT.*

GOOD LORD, THAT HARDLY SOUNDS LIKE A BATTLE WORTH FIGHTING.

I WAS THINKING ABOUT REPLACING OUR PIRATES WITH THOSE "DAUGHTERS OF THE AMAZON" WE KEEP HEARING ABOUT.

THE ONES WHO SUPPOSEDLY TORCHED ALL THE SPERM BANKS?

I'M NOT SURE HOW KEEN DONNA REED AND FRIENDS WOULD BE TO SEE A BUNCH OF ONE-TITTED LESBIAN WARRIORS PRANCING AROUND STAGE. BESIDES, I THOUGHT THE AMAZONS WERE JUST ANOTHER URBAN LEGEND.

THAT'S ALL *ANY-ONE* WANTS THESE DAYS! DON'T THEY UNDERSTAND, THE ONLY WAY WE'RE EVER GOING TO *ESCAPE* THE ABSOLUTE FUCK-ING HORROR OF THE SITUATION WE'RE IN IS TO *CONFRONT* IT!

WE DON'T NEED ART THAT *PACIFIES,* WE NEED ART THAT *CHALLENGES* AND--

YEAH...YEAH, YOU'RE PROBABLY RIGHT.

DON'T BREAK YOUR BACK FOR THESE WOMEN, CAYCE. YOU HEARD THE LADY, THEY JUST WANT A LITTLE *ESCAPISM.*

AIEEEEEE

OH, PRECIOUS, IT WAS PROBABLY JUST ONE OF OUR **HORSES**.

NUH-UH! I **KNOW** WHAT HORSES SOUND LIKE!

THIS WAS SOMETHING **BAD.** I THINK IT WAS THE... THE THING THAT KILLED ALL THE BOYS.

MANDA, A **MONSTER** DIDN'T MAKE THE MEN DIE.

THEN WHAT DID?

GOD?

AH...

WE STILL DON'T **KNOW,** MANDA. NO ONE DOES.

IT'S A...A MYSTERY.

THAT'S NOT TRUE.

I KNOW WHAT CAUSED THE PLAGUE.

WHAT ARE YOU SUGGESTING, THAT THE BLACK DEATH WAS SOME KIND OF *PUNISHMENT*... FOR KEEPING WOMEN OUT OF *THEATER*?

THINK ABOUT IT, A LOT OF ANTHROPOLOGISTS OR WHATEVER BELIEVE THAT THE FIRST PERFORMERS WERE WOMEN, RIGHT? DRAMA IS IN OUR *BLOOD*.

SO STOPPING US FROM ACTING IS UNNATURAL, AND SCREWING WITH THE NATURAL ORDER ALWAYS MESSES SHIT UP.

BUT WHAT ABOUT *OUR* PLAGUE? THERE WAS NOTHING PREVENTING ANY OF *US* FROM ACTING WHEN IT HAPPENED.

BULL*SHIT*! HOW MANY GOOD ROLES WERE OUT THERE FOR WOMEN YOUR AGE BEFORE ALL THE MEN *DIED*, HENRIETTA?

WELL...

HOW MANY GOOD ROLES WERE OUT THERE FOR *ANY* OF US? UNLESS YOU WERE NINETEEN, WILLING TO SHOW YOUR BOOBS, AND/OR JULIA ROBERTS, WHAT DID WE HAVE?

I'M NOT SAYING I'M HAPPY THAT ANYBODY CROAKED, BUT IF YOU ASK ME, THIS WHOLE CATASTROPHE WAS JUST MOTHER NATURE'S WAY OF EVENING THE SCORE.

THAT IS THE MOST OUTRAGEOUS, EGOCENTRIC, *STUPID* THING I HAVE EVER--

HRRRREEE

I...I THINK IT'S *BACK*.

HENRIETTA, GET MANDA INSIDE MY TENT. EDIE, YOU'RE WITH ME.

THE REST OF YOU, HOLD YOUR GROUND.

BOOYAH.

WHAT DO YOU THINK WE'RE DEALING WITH HERE, BOSS?

HELL IF I KNOW... THEY HAVE *BANSHEES* IN NEBRASKA?

HEY, ISN'T THAT A *PROP GUN?*

JESUS, EDIE, WHY DON'T YOU PROJECT THAT INFORMATION A LITTLE LOUDER?

RHEEEE

THERE!

WHERE?

OKAY, LADIES, YOU'VE ALL HAD A CHANCE TO GAWK AT OUR NEW MASCOT. CALL IS AT EIGHT A.M. SHARP TOMORROW, SO LET'S GET SOME SHUTEYE.

AND NO MORE BAD THOUGHTS TONIGHT, RIGHT, KIDDO?

I GUESS...

WHAT'S THE PROGNOSIS, DR. DOLITTLE?

MUCH BETTER NOW THAT THE BEAST AND I ARE BOTH PROPERLY *PISSED.*

SERIOUSLY, STITCHING MONKEY FLESH BACK TOGETHER IS A WALK IN THE PARK COMPARED TO SEWING NINETEEN BLOODY *PIRATE COSTUMES* OUT OF THIN AIR.

WHAT DO YOU THINK HAPPENED, HANK? WAS SHE ATTACKED BY A DOG OR SOMETHING?

I SINCERELY DOUBT IT. THE CUT WAS CLEAN, BUT DEEP...LIKE SOMEONE OUT THERE TOOK A SWING AT HER WITH A *BUTCHER'S KNIFE* OR SOMETHING.

GREAT, SO MUCH FOR "NO MORE BAD THOUGHTS."

OUR ONLY CONCERN RIGHT NOW SHOULD BE THIS ANIMAL'S *STENCH.* WE DON'T HAVE ANY *MONKEY NAPPIES* IN WARDROBE, DO WE?

HOLD ON, THAT'S NOT A *REAL* DIAPER. IT'S JUST AN OLD *HANDKERCHIEF.*

IF IT'S MONOGRAMMED, MAYBE WE CAN FIND OUT WHO SHE BELONGED TO...

EWW. UNLESS THE OWNER'S NAME WAS *BROWN,* I DON'T THINK WE'RE GOING TO FIND ANY CLUES IN HERE. POOR GIRL HASN'T BEEN CHANGED IN DAYS.

ACTUALLY, I'M NOT SO SURE THIS POOR GIRL...*IS* A GIRL.

WHAT THE HELL DOES *THAT* MEAN?

SEE FOR YOURSELF.

I'M HARDLY AN EXPERT, BUT I'M FAIRLY CERTAIN THAT THIS CREATURE HAS *MALE* PLUMBING.

HOLY CRAP, SHE'S *RIGHT.*

THAT'S *IMPOSSIBLE.* MONKEYS PROBABLY JUST HAVE WEIRD ANATOMIES. MAYBE THAT'S AN ENLARGED CLITORIS OR--

EE EEE

OH.

YEAH, NEVER SEEN A LITTLE MAN IN THE BOAT DO *THAT* BEFORE.

BUT I THOUGHT THE PLAGUE KILLED *EVERY* MAMMAL WITH A Y CHROMOSOME. I MEAN, I LOST BOTH MY MALE CATS. AND ALL OF MY BOYFRIEND'S *STALLIONS* DIED.

HALF OF THE MICE IN MY APARTMENT FINALLY PASSED ON, AND I'D BEEN TRYING TO KILL THEM FOR *YEARS.*

SO THE PLAGUE AFFECTED EVERYTHING BUT *MONKEYS?* HOW THE FUCK DOES THAT MAKE ANY SENSE? ISN'T THEIR *DNA*, LIKE, ALMOST IDENTICAL TO OURS?

LORD, WHAT IF IT *DID* AFFECT MONKEYS...JUST NOT *THIS* ONE?

WHAT IF THIS IS THE *LAST MALE* ON EARTH?

YOU'RE STARTING TO SOUND LIKE *EDIE,* HENRIETTA.

THAT STILL MAKES THIS AN *ENORMOUS* DISCOVERY. WE HAVE TO TELL--

BUBBLES HERE IS PROBABLY JUST SOME KIND OF FREAK ANOMALY...LIKE THE HANDFUL OF PEOPLE WHO ARE SUPPOSEDLY IMMUNE TO *HIV* INFECTION, YOU KNOW?

NO! THIS STAYS BETWEEN THE THREE OF US.

IF WORD SPREADS, WOMEN MIGHT START HOLDING OUT HOPE THAT A *HUMAN* MALE IS ALIVE SOME- WHERE, TOO.

WHAT'S SO BAD ABOUT GIVING PEOPLE A LITTLE HOPE?

IT'S IRRESPONSIBLE! THE PROMISE OF SOME IMAGINARY LAST MAN WHO MIGHT COME ALONG AND... AND *SAVE US* JUST GIVES WOMEN ANOTHER EXCUSE TO BE *COMPLACENT.*

WE'RE GOING TO BE *GONE* WITHIN A GENERATION IF WE DON'T GET OFF OUR ASSES AND FIND A WAY TO SAVE *OUR- SELVES!* *THAT'S* THE MESSAGE OUR TROUPE IS SUPPOSED TO BE SPREADING!

HOW...BY PUTTING ON *PIRATE MUSICALS?*

I'M SORRY, CAYCE, BUT--

NO. YOU'RE... YOU'RE ABSOLUTELY RIGHT.

SO...WE *ARE* GOING TO TELL THE OTHERS?

NO. WE'RE GOING TO DO A *PLAY* ABOUT IT.

A PLAY ABOUT A *MONKEY?*

A PLAY ABOUT THE LAST MAN ON EARTH.

AN ORIGINAL WORK?

WHY NOT? I'M GOING TO WRITE SOMETHING SET RIGHT HERE, RIGHT NOW...A STORY ABOUT A GROUP OF WOMEN WHO DISCOVER THE ONLY LIVING MAN.

IS THAT REALLY SUCH A GOOD IDEA, LUV? WON'T IT SEEM LIKE WE'RE EXPLOITING TRAGEDY FOR, WELL... THE PURPOSES OF *ENTERTAINMENT?*

BUT THIS WILL BE *MORE* THAN ENTERTAINMENT! THIS WILL BE *ART!* WE'LL BE USING FICTION TO...TO HELP US GET TO THE *TRUTH!*

IT'S THE PERFECT STORY TO CONVEY ALL OF THE IDEAS I'VE BEEN TRYING TO GET ACROSS ABOUT LIFE IN THE POST-PLAGUE WORLD!

IT'S LIKE THE GODS SENT ME MY OWN SMELLY LITTLE *MUSE.*

AND YOU CALL *ME* EGOCENTRIC...

Afternoon.

A Kitchen: A table, a chair, a jar of pickled artichoke hearts.

A lone figure enters.

This is **TERESA**, one of billions of women made a widow by the Plague.

But unlike so many of her friends, Teresa hasn't turned to drugs or alcohol, she hasn't contemplated suicide. She is a pillar of strength, an independent woman.

Because Teresa and her husband built a shelter in their basement after 9/11, she has enough food to last her more than a year.

Teresa will not die. She is a **survivor**.

But as she sits down to enjoy her lunch, Teresa is confronted with a problem…

She is unable to open the jar.

She strains and struggles, but to no avail.

That's when it hits her... opening jars was the one thing she always asked her **husband** to do.

She and her friends used to joke that it was the **only** thing men were good for.

And then, the enormity of the situation sets in.

Teresa realizes that her husband is never coming back.

None of the men are coming back.

She reacts the same way the rest of us did when **we** finally allowed this moment to happen.

AHHHHHHH!

KERAASH

Just then a singsong voice calls out:

♪IT'S SO NICE TO HAVE A MAN AROUND THE HOUSE...♪

DAMMIT, EDIE! PLEASE DON'T BREAK CHARACTER. WE RUINED A REAL JAR OF FOOD FOR THIS REHEARSAL!

AND WHERE'S THE REST OF YOUR COSTUME? YOU LOOK LIKE AN AD FOR *CHICKS WITH DICKS*.

RR ROO ROO

SORRY, CAYCE, BUT IT'S A MILLION FUCKING DEGREES IN HERE.

AND SERIOUSLY, IS THERE ANY CHANCE MY CHARACTER'S NAME COULD BE A LITTLE MORE...DRAMATIC? HOW ABOUT SOMETHING SHAKESPEARIAN? LIKE HAMLET OR...OR *ROMEO*!

IF THERE'S ONE THING I HATE, IT'S CRAPPY WORKS OF FICTION THAT TRY TO SOUND IMPORTANT BY STEALING NAMES FROM THE *BARD*.

BESIDES, LIONEL IS MY TRIBUTE TO THE FOUNDING MOTHER OF SCI-FI...A LITTLE TIP OF THE HAT TO *MARY SHELLEY*.

149

THE FRANKENSTEIN CHICK?

BACK IN THE 1800'S, SHE WROTE THIS BOOK CALLED *THE LAST MAN*, ABOUT A TWENTY-FIRST CENTURY PLAGUE THAT KILLS EVERYONE EXCEPT FOR A GUY NAMED LIONEL.

FUCK... WHAT CAUSED IT?

THE PLAGUE? SHE NEVER REALLY GETS AROUND TO EXPLAINING IT. BUT IT'S NOT THE POINT OF HER STORY.

IT'S A CONDEMNATION OF THE... THE UNCHECKED *MASCULINITY* THAT WAS ALWAYS THREATENING TO DESTROY THE PLANET.

IT'S ABOUT THE FAILURE OF ART AND IMAGINATION TO SAVE THE WORLD.

WELL, THAT'S ALL VERY NICE, BUT I STILL DON'T UNDERSTAND *MY* CHARACTER'S MOTIVATION.

I MEAN, IF TERESA CAN'T OPEN THE JAR, WHY DOESN'T SHE JUST USE A PAIR OF LATEX DISHWASHING GLOVES? YOU GET A REAL NICE GRIP THAT WAY, AND IT MAKES IT SUPER-EASY TO--

NO KIDDING! BUT THIS ISN'T THE GODDAMN MARTHA STEWART HOUR! WE'RE NOT HERE TO GIVE HELPFUL HOUSEHOLD TIPS! THIS IS *DRAMA!* TERESA'S DILEMMA IS AN *ALLEGORY!*

JESUS, WHY IS EVERYONE ACTING LIKE THIS IS THEIR *FIRST* FUCKING PLAY?

CAYCE, LUV, PERHAPS NOW WOULD BE A GOOD TIME FOR A SHORT BREAK? YOU COULD PROBABLY DO WITH SOME FRESH AIR.

...FINE.

BUT SOMEBODY SWEEP UP THOSE ARTICHOKES. MAYBE *CURIOUS GEORGETTE* HERE CAN EAT THEM FOR LUNCH.

MM MNN

CAYCE, BE GENTLE WITH THE GIRLS. THEY'VE BEEN WORKING TO GET OFF-BOOK ALL MORNING.

FOR GOD'S SAKE, YOU WROTE THIS PIECE IN LESS THAN A *NIGHT*.

I DIDN'T WRITE IT, HENRIETTA. IT WROTE ITSELF.

EXACTLY. YOU'VE BEEN ACTING LIKE A WOMAN POSSESSED EVER SINCE WE FOUND THIS ANIMAL. HE'S TURNED YOU INTO--

SHHHH!

RIGHT NOW, YOU, EDIE AND I ARE THE ONLY THREE PEOPLE ALIVE WHO KNOW THAT OUR MONKEY IS ACTUALLY A *HE*.

IF ANYONE ELSE FINDS OUT THAT WE STUMBLED ONTO A LIVING *MALE*, MASS HYSTERIA WILL SWEEP THROUGH NEBRASKA LIKE A FUCKING--

WHAT IS GOING *ON* HERE?

YOU'RE DOING A PLAY ABOUT A **MAN** WHO SURVIVED THE PLAGUE?

THAT'S RIGHT, MA'AM. WE--

WHEN I AGREED TO LET YOU PEOPLE USE OUR THEATER, YOU TOLD ME THAT YOU WOULD FIND SOMETHING **APPROPRIATE** TO PERFORM.

WELL, WHAT IN HEAVEN'S NAME IS APPROPRIATE ABOUT **YOUR** IDEA? OUR **SUFFERING** SHOULDN'T BE FODDER FOR YOUR...YOUR CRUEL **FLIGHTS OF FANCY**!

PERHAPS YOU MIGHT WAIT TO **SEE** THE SHOW BEFORE YOU PASS JUDGMENT?

I DON'T NEED TO! THE WOMEN OF NORTHLAKE WANT OLD-FASHIONED ENTERTAINMENT, NOT THIS KIND OF CRASS EXPLOITATION!

REALLY? BECAUSE THE FIRST TWO EVENINGS OF THIS "CRASS EXPLOITATION" ARE ALREADY COMPLETELY SOLD OUT.

I ASSURE YOU, WE HAVE NO INTENTION OF DISRESPECTING THE FATHERS, HUSBANDS, SONS AND BROTHERS THAT YOU--THAT **WE**--ALL LOST.

THIS IS A PROVOCATIVE PLAY, BUT IT'S ALL DONE IN VERY GOOD TASTE.

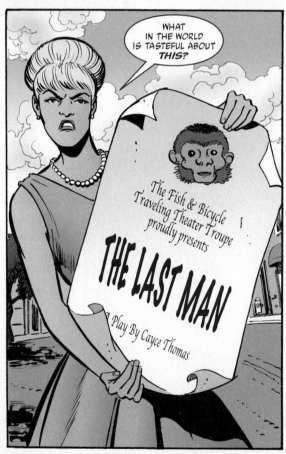

WHAT IN THE WORLD IS TASTEFUL ABOUT **THIS**?

The Fish & Bicycle Traveling Theater Troupe proudly presents

THE LAST MAN

A Play By Cayce Thomas

WHAT THE FU--

ER, THAT WAS EDIE'S DOING, CAYCE. SHE THOUGHT A PICTURE OF YOUR NEW PET WOULD MAKE FOR AN INTRIGUING *TEASER* POSTER.

THESE ARE PLASTERED ALL OVER TOWN!

THIS IS HOW YOU HONOR OUR DEAD... BY COMPARING MEN TO A SMILING *CHIMP*?

OF COURSE NOT. SEE, THIS MONKEY IS SORT OF THE...THE *SYMBOL* OF OUR THEATER COMPANY. IN CHINA, THEY REPRESENT, UH, CREATIVITY AND--

WE'RE NOT INTERESTED IN YOUR PRETENTIOUS GARBAGE.

WHY DON'T YOU PEDDLE YOUR *FILTH* ELSEWHERE?

BECAUSE WE HAVE A *RIGHT* TO EXPRESS OURSELVES.

AS DO I.

AND I HAVE EVERY INTENTION OF DOING JUST THAT.

WHAT DOES *THAT* MEAN?

IGNORE HER, CAYCE.

WHEN I DID THAT PLAY ABOUT A GAY JESUS, EVERY BLOODY SOCCER MOM WITH A PLACARD CAME OUT TO--

ARK ARK ARK

IT'S BEEN *TWO MONTHS.* I WAS SURE--

YOU HAVE TO BELIEVE ME, I WAS IN AN *ELEVATOR* WHEN THE PLAGUE HIT AND...AND THE ELECTRICITY WENT OUT.

I STILL DON'T UNDERSTAND HOW I SURVIVED. THE OTHER TWO MEN I WAS WITH, THEY...THEY JUST SEEMED TO *BURST.*

TERESA, I WAS *TRAPPED* IN THAT BLACK BOX WITH THEIR ROTTING CORPSES. GOD FORGIVE ME, I...I HAD TO FEED ON THEIR *FLESH* TO STAY ALIVE.

I WAS TEMPTED TO JUST GIVE IN...BUT THE MEMORY OF YOUR FACE KEPT ME GOING. AND FINALLY, LAST NIGHT, SOMEONE HEARD MY CRIES AND--

THIS IS REAL? THIS...THIS IS REALLY *HAPPENING?*

CLAP CLAP CLAP CLAP CLAP CLAP

WELL, THIS IS GOING BETTER THAN EXPECTED.

AND NARY A SINGLE PROTESTOR OUTSIDE.

WE'RE NOT OUT OF THE WOODS YET. I MEAN, WE'RE STILL GIVING THE AUDIENCE WHAT THEY WANT. WAIT FOR US TO START *SUBVERTING* THEIR FANTASIES AFTER INTERMISSION...

GOOD SHOW OUT THERE, EDIE. YOU SOUND MORE LIKE A MAN THAN LEO DICAPRIO EVER DID.

WHATEVER, I'M DONE KISSING CHICKS IN PLAYS, THAT'S FOR SURE. MY CO-STARS KEEP "ACCIDENTALLY" SLIPPING ME THE TONGUE.

CAN YOU BLAME THEM? YOU'RE ALMOST CONVINCING ENOUGH TO MAKE *ME* WET... AND I'M THE ONE WHO SPIRIT-GUMMED THAT THING TO YOUR FACE.

NNN

SERIOUSLY, THIS IS ACTUALLY THE BEST I'VE FELT ABOUT A ROLE IN FOREVER, CAYCE. WE SHOULD THINK ABOUT TAKING THIS ONE ON THE ROAD.

YES, BREAK A LEG OUT THERE, LUV.

LET'S SEE IF WE CAN SURVIVE ACT TWO FIRST, ALL RIGHT?

IF ANYONE ELSE TRIES TO FRENCH ME, I'LL BREAK A LOT MORE THAN *THAT*!

⟨DR. M, THIS IS TOYOTA.⟩

⟨I'M AFRAID WE HAVE A PROBLEM.⟩

⟨YOU'VE LOST THE ANIMAL AGAIN?⟩

⟨NO, I'M RIGHT THE FUCK ON TOP OF IT. UNFORTUNATELY, SO ARE A BUNCH OF CIVVIES...PRETTY MUCH PERPETUALLY.⟩

⟨I CAN RETRIEVE THE PACKAGE, BUT I CAN'T GUARANTEE THAT I WON'T OFF A FEW FRIENDLIES IN THE PROCESS.⟩

⟨DAMMIT. THE LAST THING I NEED IS MORE BLOOD ON MY HANDS...⟩

⟨STILL, I CAN'T GUARANTEE THAT WHATEVER GENETIC MATERIAL YOU WERE ALREADY ABLE TO CARVE OUT OF THE BEAST WILL BE ENOUGH.⟩

⟨STAY IN POSITION FOR ANOTHER HOUR, TOYOTA. BUT ONLY MAKE A MOVE IF YOU CAN LIMIT THE NUMBER OF CASUALTIES TO NO MORE THAN ONE. I CAN'T JUSTIFY ANOTHER BODY COUNT.⟩

HAI, DOMO ARIGATO...

⟨...YOU TIME-WASTING ASSHOLE.⟩

⟨IF THERE'S ONE THING I HATE SITTING THROUGH, IT'S FUCKING THEATER...⟩

I'VE SEEN *ENOUGH!*

THIS PLAY IS A *MOCKERY!*

SIT DOWN!

NO, SHE'S RIGHT!

IT'S *OBSCENE!*

BE QUIET!

ARE WE REALLY GOING TO LET THESE PEOPLE PORTRAY WOMEN AS PETTY, VICIOUS *TRAMPS?*

YOU JUST INTERRUPTED MY FIGHT SCENE...

...YOU FUCKING *BITCH!*

LISTEN UP!

WE'RE LOOKING FOR THE CAPUCHIN MONKEY PICTURED HERE!

The Fish & Bicycle Traveling Theater Troupe proudly presents

THE LAST MAN

A Play By Cayce Thomas

WHY?

WHO *ARE* YOU PEOPLE?

WE'RE WITH W.H.O.

THAT'S RIGHT, THE WORLD HEALTH ORGANIZATION.

WHO?

AW, YOU GOT TO IT TOO FAST, 355. YOU WERE FOUR LINES AWAY FROM AN ABBOTT AND COSTELLO ROUTINE.

THAT ANIMAL IS A PUBLIC HEALTH RISK.

I'LL HAVE TO ASK YOU TO GIVE IT BACK TO US.

ABSOLUTELY NOT!

WE PATCHED UP WHATEVER YOU MONSTERS DID TO HIM. HE BELONGS TO *US* NOW.

HE?

163

OH. IT'S NOT REALLY A BOY.

IT'S A, UH, FEMALE WITH MALE GENITALIA... LIKE THAT ACTRESS, *WHAT'S-HER-NAME.*

I BEG YOUR PARDON!

WHICH ACTRESS WOULD *THAT* BE?

OH, NOT ONE OF *YOU,* THE ONE FROM ALL THOSE HORROR--

WHAT MY ASSOCIATE *MEANT* TO SAY IS THAT WE'VE BEEN WORKING ON GENETICALLY ENGINEERING A NEW BREED OF, UH...PLAGUE-RESISTANT *HERMAPHRODITES.*

UNFORTUNATELY, THE SPECIMENS WE'VE CREATED SO FAR--LIKE THE MONKEY THAT ESCAPED OUR FACILITY--MIGHT ALSO BE CARRIERS OF A...A HIGHLY CONTAGIOUS *ASIAN FLU.*

OH.

IN THAT CASE...

WELCOME BACK, SHIT-SLINGER.

THAT'S THE LAST TIME WE TRUST *YORICK* TO KEEP AN EYE ON YOU.

HEY, I *TOLD* YOU, DR. MANN, WHEN I WOKE UP, AMPERSAND'S TRAVELING CASE WAS EMPTY, AND SOME *NINJA CHICK* WAS JUMPING OUT OF OUR TRAIN CAR.

NINJA CHICK. RIIIIGHT...

THANK YOU FOR YOUR COOPERATION.

I APOLOGIZE FOR INTERRUPTING YOUR... PERFORMANCE.

HEY, IS THIS PLAY REALLY ABOUT THE LAST GUY ON EARTH?

DON'T WORRY, MA'AM, WE'VE ALREADY SHUT IT DOWN.

WHY DON'T I SHUT DOWN YOUR FAT *FACE*, DOUCHE NOZZLE?

YES, THIS WORK DOES INDEED DEAL WITH A GENTLEMAN SURVIVOR, AND THE PRODUCTION IS GOING TO HAVE A LONG, SUCCESSFUL RUN IN EVERY *OPEN-MINDED* CITY IN THE COUNTRY.

CAYCE HERE IS THE AUTHOR.

I WAS JUST WONDERING...HOW DOES IT END?

Cleveland, Ohio
Fifteen Years Ago

169

YOU KNOW HE GETS CONFUSED IF WE ALL TRY TO TALK WITH HIM AT THE SAME--

I DON'T CARE!

I...I DON'T EVEN *LIKE* HIM! HE ALWAYS TRIES TO TOUCH MY--

IT'S OKAY, DAD.

I CAN GO IN FIRST.

THERE'S A BRAVE SOLDIER.

HE DIDN'T EVEN NEED A ST. CRISPIN'S DAY SPEECH TO GET *HIM* INTO THE FRONT LINE.

I HOPE YOU BOTH GET *AIDS.*

EXIT

HELLO?

GRAMPY...?

IT'S ME. YORICK.

YORICK *WHO?*

HA HA, HILARIOUS.

COME HERE, YA LITTLE BASTARD. WHAT BRINGS YOU TO THIS DUMP?

MOM'S IN TOWN FOR CAMPAIGN STUFF, REMEMBER?

HEY, HOW COME THERE ARE SO MANY WOMEN IN HERE?

WHY?

'CAUSE WOMEN LIVE LONGER THAN MEN.

'CAUSE THEY SUCK ALL THE GODDAMN *LIFE* OUT OF US.

OH.

WELL, IT MUST BE COOL TO BE, LIKE, THE ONLY GUY WITH SO MANY GIRLS ALL OVER THE PLACE.

YOU *CRAZY?* IT'S HELL ON EARTH! AIN'T *NOTHING* WORSE THAN LADIES IN NUMBERS.

SOMEDAY, YOU'LL UNDERSTAND...

Allenspark, Colorado
Now

SPAK

DOC!

I'LL TAKE CARE OF HER! GO! HIDE IN THE WOODS.

BUT AMPERSAND--

I'VE GOT HIM, JUST *RUN* ALREADY!

DR. MANN?

ALLISON? ARE YOU...?

I'M...I'M ALL RIGHT, 355.

I TOLD YOU THESE DORKY THINGS SAVE...

...LIVES?

TELL US WHERE THE THIRD GAL IN YOUR LITTLE RAIDING PARTY WENT OFF TO...OR WE START SHOOTING MORE THAN TIRES.

I THINK YOUR EYES WERE PLAYING TRICKS ON YOU, SHERIFF. THERE ARE ONLY TWO OF US, AND WE *AREN'T* HERE TO STEAL YOUR CATTLE.

WE'RE TRYING TO REACH ST. JOSEPH'S HOSPITAL IN DENVER SO WE CAN GET SOME ANTIBIOTICS FOR OUR *PET*.

HE, UH, *SHE* GOT A BAD CUT ON HER ARM A FEW DAYS BACK, AND I'M PRETTY SURE IT'S *INFECTED*. BUT IF WE HAD KNOWN THIS WAS PRIVATE PROPERTY--

AIN'T NOTHING PRIVATE ABOUT IT. LAND BARONS WENT EXTINCT SAME TIME ALL THE FELLAS DID. THIS EARTH BELONGS TO ANY WOMAN WANTS TO SET FOOT ON IT.

ANY WOMAN 'CEPT *AMAZONS*, THAT IS.

AMAZONS?

I'M AFRAID YOU'RE CONFUSED. I'M ACTUALLY--

UHN!

THAT WAS... *UNNECESSARY.*

176

I WAS SIMPLY REACHING FOR IDENTIFICATION. I'M A *FEDERAL AGENT.*

FEDERAL AGENT OF *WHAT?*

TECHNICALLY, MY ORGANIZATION IS CLASSIFIED, BUT THE PRESIDENT HAS AUTHORIZED ME TO--

SAVE THAT BULLSHIT FOR THE MAGISTRATES.

YEAH, WE BEEN WARNED ABOUT YOUR KIND...MUTILATIN' YOUR OWN TEATS, TEARING AROUND ON MOTORCYCLES, STEALING FOOD FROM DEFENSELESS WOMEN.

YOU PEOPLE HAVE NO *CLUE* WHAT YOU'RE TALKING ABOUT.

WE'RE *NOT* DAUGHTERS OF THE AMAZON!

PROVE IT. SHOW US YOUR BREASTS.

WHAT?

RELAX, WE'RE NOT HOMOSEXUALS.

BESIDES, IF YOU'RE TELLING THE TRUTH, YOU AIN'T GOT NOTHING WE HAVEN'T ALL SEEN--

REACH FOR THE SKY, PARDNERS!

WHAT DO I CARE?

WE BREASTLESS AMAZONS *ACHE* FOR THE SWEET EMBRACE OF MOTHER OBLIVION.

SAY *WHAT?*

GIRL AIN'T RIGHT IN THE HEAD.

BUTTERCUP!

LAST CHANCE, HAND OVER YOUR WEAPONS TO MY ASSOCIATES.

THREE... *TWO*...

ALL RIGHT, ALL RIGHT!

JUST... JUST TAKE HER EASY.

BITCH.

NOW THEN.

YOU'VE GOT ABOUT A TWO-HOUR WALK BACK TO CIVILIZATION.

I'LL LEAVE YOUR WEAPONS WITH THE FIRST REPUTABLE TRADING POST WE PASS.

YOU MEAN... YOU WOMEN *AIN'T* AMAZONS?

DO *THESE* LOOK MUTILATED TO YOU, YOU IGNORANT *SHITHEADS?*

JEEZ.

SO MUCH FOR PROTECTING A LADY'S *DIGNITY...*

OROOOOOO

FUCK, I THINK AMPERSAND'S GETTING WORSE, 355. ARE WE ALMOST THERE?

YOU'RE NOT GOING TO THE HOSPITAL, YORICK. NOT AFTER THAT CRAP YOU PULLED BACK THERE.

WHAT? I SAVE YOUR LIVES, AND YOU PUNISH MY *MONKEY?* HE'S GONNA *DIE* WITHOUT MEDICINE!

YOU DIDN'T SAVE OUR LIVES, YOU NEEDLESSLY RISKED YOUR OWN... *AGAIN.*

ANYWAY, DR. MANN AND I ARE STILL TAKING AMPERSAND TO ST. JOSEPH'S. WE'RE JUST NOT BRINGING *YOU* WITH US.

IF THAT PONY EXPRESS CHICK WE MET IN NEBRASKA WAS TELLING THE TRUTH, ST. JOE'S IS GUARDED LIKE AREA 51.

GETTING MY HANDS ON MORE AUGMENTIN IS GOING TO TAKE PATIENCE, DIPLOMACY AND FINESSE.

QUALITIES YOU'VE NEVER EVEN *HEARD* OF.

SO YOU'RE... YOU'RE JUST GOING TO *LEAVE* ME?

NOT BY YOURSELF.

I DIDN'T WANT TO DO THIS, BUT I HAVE A COLLEAGUE WHO LIVES A FEW MILES FROM HERE.

A CULPER RING AGENT?

EX-CULPER.

SHE TOOK A PERMANENT LEAVE OF ABSENCE AFTER HER HUSBAND-SLASH-PARTNER WAS ASSASSINATED BY *17 NOVEMBER.*

WAIT, I DON'T WANT TO STAY WITH SOME SHELL-SHOCKED *WIDOW!* PLEASE! I PROMISE, I'LL BE ON MY BEST BEHAVIOR! I--

YORICK, I'VE KNOWN THIS WOMAN SINCE SHE WAS *NINE.* WE WERE IN THE SAME ORPHANAGE WHEN WE WERE BOTH RECRUITED.

AGENT 711 HAS SAVED MY ASS ALMOST AS OFTEN AS I'VE SAVED HERS. YOU'LL BE FINE.

HOLD ON, HER CODENAME IS SERIOUSLY *711?* MAN, HOW MANY GUYS USED TO ASK IF SHE'S "OPEN ALL NIGHT"?

711 WAS *GENERAL WASHINGTON'S* CODENAME DURING THE REVOLUTIONARY WAR. THAT DESIGNATION WAS AWARDED TO MY FRIEND AFTER SHE HELPED SAVE THE WORLD FROM NUCLEAR ANNIHILATION.

IF YOU MAKE A SINGLE CRACK AT HER EXPENSE, I WILL RIP OFF YOUR PENIS WITH A CLAW HAMMER.

SADDLE UP.

182

OH MY GOD. *355?*

LONG TIME, 711.

1033?

HE'S DEAD. 241 AND 853, TOO. *ALL* OF THE PRIMES, OBVIOUSLY.

I CAN'T IMAGINE, 355. I'M STILL NOT OVER 1451.

WE LIVE IN PROFOUNDLY STRANGE TIMES.

YEP.

"711, THESE ARE MY NEW CHARGES."

"MY FRIENDS."

"DR. ALLISON MANN, BIOENGINEER OUT OF BOSTON. IF ANYONE CAN FIGURE OUT WHAT CAUSED THE PLAGUE, IT'S HER."

"PLEASURE."

"MN."

"AND THIS, AS FAR AS WE KNOW, IS THE LAST MAN ON EARTH."

"HIYA."

"IS...IS THIS SOME KIND OF JOKE?"

"THAT'S WHAT I KEEP ASKING MYSELF."

"HOW?"

"DOES...DOES THIS HAVE SOMETHING TO DO WITH THE AMULET OF HELENE?"

"AH, ACTUALLY, MAYBE WE SHOULD SPEAK IN PRIVATE, 711..."

WELL, SHE SEEMS... *NICE.*

REMINDS ME OF ONE OF MY *EXES.* DUMPED ME THE NIGHT BEFORE MY FUCKING *MCAT.*

HOLD ON, *SHE* REMINDS YOU OF AN EX-*BOYFRIEND?*

THAT'S NOT WHAT I SAID.

YES, YOU DID! YOU JUST...

GET OUT!

YOU'RE TELLING ME I'VE BEEN TRAVELING WITH YOU FOR A *YEAR,* AND I NEVER EVEN FIGURED OUT THAT YOU WERE... YOU KNOW...

YES, WELL, I SUPPOSE WE CAN ADD *GAYDAR* TO THE EXTRAORDINARY NUMBER OF COMMON SENSES YOU SEEM TO LACK.

ALL RIGHT, DOCTOR, I THINK WE'RE READY TO RIDE.

711 HAS KINDLY OFFERED TO LOOK AFTER YORICK UNTIL WE RETURN.

COME BACK WITH A HEALTHY MONKEY, OR DON'T COME BACK AT ALL.

LIKE YOU COULD LIVE WITHOUT *ME.*

BE GOOD, 'RICK.

I'VE LEFT MY JOURNALS WITH 711, JUST SO SHE KNOWS WHAT SHE'LL BE DEALING WITH.

YOU... YOU KEEP A *JOURNAL?*

WHY DON'T YOU COME INSIDE, MR. BROWN?

I HAVE SOMETHING YOU MIGHT LIKE TO SEE.

HOLY CRAP!

IT'S PARADISE CITY!

THEY BELONGED TO MY HUSBAND. YOU'RE WELCOME TO BORROW AS MANY AS YOU LIKE.

YOU ARE A *GODDESS*. WHEN I LEFT BROOKLYN, ALL I TOOK WITH ME WAS A COPY OF *ZEN AND THE ART OF MOTORCYCLE MAINTENANCE*. IT'S MY GIRLFRIEND BETH'S FAVORITE BOOK, BUT I HAVE A SHORT ATTENTION SPAN FOR--

HEY, *THE DAY OF THE LOCUST*.

THIS IS THE GREATEST NOVEL OF ALL TIME!

IS THAT NATHANIEL WEST? NEVER READ HIM. I'VE ALWAYS PREFERRED *POETRY* TO PROSE.

OH, IT'S GOT THE MOST HILARIOUS CHARACTER EVER, THIS GUY NAMED *HOMER SIMPSON*.

AND THIS WAS WRITTEN ABOUT FIFTY YEARS BEFORE THE CARTOON, MIND YOU.

HOMER'S THIS AWKWARD, NAÏVE SHUT-IN WHO'S UNCOMFORTABLE WITH HIS OWN SEXUALITY, BUT HE LEAVES HIS LIFE OF SOLITUDE TO GO TO CALIFORNIA.

AND WHAT DOES HE HOPE TO FIND THERE, YORICK?

Yorick, you need to wake up.

189

Where the Hell Am I?

I DON'T GET IT.

YOU AND THREE-FIFTY ARE SUPPOSED TO BE PART OF THE SAME STUPID CLUB.

WE ARE. BUT THE SUM TOTAL OF WHAT AGENT 355 DOESN'T KNOW ABOUT THE *TRUE* CULPER RING COULD JUST ABOUT FILL THE *MARIANAS TRENCH.*

THAT WOMAN HAS NO IDEA WHO WE *REALLY* ARE.

GAH!

WHAT ARE YOU SCREAMING ABOUT NOW, *FAG?*

WHY...WHY DO YOU KEEP CALLING ME THAT? I'M *STRAIGHT.*

BULLSHIT. I READ 355'S JOURNALS. YOU'VE BEEN THE ONLY MAN ON EARTH FOR *MONTHS,* AND YOU HAVEN'T HAD SEX WITH *ONE* GIRL YET.

YOU HAVEN'T EVEN *SEEN* PUSSY!

SO...TELL ME ABOUT THE FIRST TIME YOU FUCKED ANOTHER BOY.

THWAP

AHN!

YOU HAPPY, ASSHOLE? YOU THINK YOU DISCOVERED MY ROSEBUD OR SOMETHING?

IT WAS SICK KID BULLSHIT. I TOLD MY PARENTS. I SAW A FUCKING SHRINK. IT WAS NOTHING. IT'S NOT MY SECRET ORIGIN.

METHINKS SHE DOTH PROTEST...

IS THAT WHY YOU BECAME AN ESCAPE ARTIST?

SO YOU COULD GET FREE IF SOMETHING LIKE THAT EVER HAPPENED AGAIN?

OR IS IT BECAUSE YOU LIKE REMEMBERING THE WAY IT *FELT?*

YOU WANT TO KNOW THE TRUTH...?

YOUR HIPS ARE *HUGE,* YOU FUCKING COW.

FINE.

IF THAT'S HOW WE'RE GOING TO DO THINGS...

WAIT, WHAT'S THAT?

WHAT ARE YOU--

GHHHH!

NOW. WHY DON'T YOU TELL ME ABOUT YOUR FIRST TIME...WITH A MEMBER OF THE OPPOSITE SEX, THAT IS.

NO! THAT'S MINE!

YOU CAN'T HAVE THAT! YOU... YOU...

...beth...

I WAS A SOPHOMORE AND A VIRGIN BUT SHE WAS JUST A SOPHOMORE AND WE'D BEEN FRIENDS SINCE ORIENTATION BUT STARTED HOOKING UP WITH EACH OTHER AFTER

SHE GOT DUMPED BY ONE OF MY ROOMMATES AND WE PROMISED NOT TO FALL IN LOVE BUT THEN WE DID BY ACCIDENT AND SHE MOVED OUT OF THE DORMS ON

PURPOSE AND GOT HER OWN SHITTY STUDIO APARTMENT IN THE EAST VILLAGE BETWEEN A SUSHI RESTAURANT AND A PIZZA JOINT AND I SAID SHE WAS COMPLETING THE

AXIS BECAUSE SHE'S GERMAN AND WE WERE GONNA WAIT UNTIL SHE WAS ON THE PILL BUT THEN SHE GAVE ME THIS *LOOK* THAT BURNED INTO MY MIND AND THEN

The next morning, I saw the most horrifying thing I've ever seen.

I woke up before Beth, and noticed something on her floor. It was the tissues I had tossed aside just before we collapsed. They had turned **black**...

...black with **flies.**

There were dozens of them, feasting on my lust, my depravity...

...my **weakness.**

204

AND NOW THEY HAD A *TASTE* FOR IT.

FOR MONTHS, I HAD THESE NIGHTMARES ABOUT MAGGOTS CRAWLING UP MY URETHRA AND...AND NESTING IN MY *TESTICLES*.

JESUS, YOU HAVE *PROBLEMS*.

MORE ALL THE TIME...

YORICK, DO YOU EVEN *LIKE* SEX?

OF...OF COURSE.

BUT YOU THINK IT'S *FILTHY*?

I DON'T KNOW. YES. *NO*.

ARE YOU ATTRACTED TO ME, YORICK?

I GUESS.

A LITTLE?

A...A LOT.

THEN WHY DON'T YOU HAVE SEX WITH *ME*?

BECAUSE...

SO, UH, MOMMY SAID THAT YOU AND I SHOULD HAVE A TALK ABOUT...YOU KNOW.

I FIGURED OUT WHAT YOU'RE DOING WITH MY TRACING PAPER, YORICK! YOU'RE DRAWING PICTURES OF GIRLS WITH NO CLOTHES ON! YOU LEFT AN IMPRINT ON MY PAD, ASS!

HERO SKETCHEZ

WELL, WE CALL THEM MORTAL SINS BECAUSE THEY DEPRIVE US OF GOD'S SANCTIFYING GRACE, THUS KILLING THE SOUL.

...BECAUSE I HAVE A GIRL-FRIEND.

YOU KNOW THAT'S NOT THE *REAL* REASON, YORICK.

THIS BETH GIRL IS ON THE OTHER SIDE OF THE *WORLD.* YOU'LL NEVER FIND HER.

YOU'RE WRONG.

SO WHAT IF I AM?

WHAT DOES *SHE* HAVE TO DO WITH *US?*

I *LOVE* HER.

YOU THINK JFK DIDN'T LOVE JACKIE? YOU THINK MLK DIDN'T LOVE CORETTA?

GREAT MEN FUCK AROUND ON THEIR WOMEN, YORICK, AND WHETHER YOU LIKE IT OR NOT, YOU'RE THE *GREATEST* MAN ALIVE NOW.

I CAN'T HAVE SEX WITH YOU.

YOU CAN'T OR YOU WON'T?

BECAUSE *CAN'T* IS A PROBLEM WE CAN DEAL WITH.

GOD, ENOUGH WITH THE FUCKING JOKES ALREADY! YOU'RE A FUCKING *CHILD!*

I'M NOT THE ONE PLAYING DRESS-UP.

AND I'M NOT THE ONE LIVING IN DENIAL!

I MEAN, A FEW MINUTES AGO, YOU ACTUALLY SAID THE MOST HORRIFYING THING YOU'VE EVER SEEN WAS A BUNCH OF INSECTS EATING YOUR *SEED!*

YORICK, YOU SURVIVED A PLAGUE THAT WIPED OUT NEARLY THREE BILLION PEOPLE!

THREE! BILLION!

DO YOU HONESTLY EXPECT ME TO BELIEVE THE WORST THING YOU'VE EVER SEEN IS A FEW *BUGS?*

FUCK YOU.

BY ALL MEANS.

GET OFF.

I'M TRYING.

I'M SERIOUS, DON'T!

YORICK, COME ON! THIS IS YOUR DUTY. YOUR SPERM IS MANKIND'S LAST HOPE.

NO! DR. MANN--

--IS A QUACK! BILLIONS OF MEN HAD CENTURIES TO MAKE A CLONE AND COULDN'T. WHAT MAKES YOU THINK ONE WOMAN WILL BE ABLE TO PULL IT OFF IN A FEW YEARS?

FACE IT, YOU'RE ALL THAT WE HAVE!

BUT AMPERSAND--

WHAT, YOU WANT ME TO MATE WITH YOUR MONKEY?

BESIDES, 355 TOLD ME THAT THING WAS MOST LIKELY GOING TO DIE BEFORE THEY EVER REACHED THE HOSPITAL.

GET ON YOUR KNEES.

SORRY, I SWORE OFF BOBBING FOR APPLES AFTER A HALLOWEEN PARTY GONE BAD IN THIRD--

DO IT!

¡UHF!

THERE'S SOMETHING YOU'RE NOT TELLING ME, YORICK.

EVER SINCE THE PLAGUE KILLED EVERY OTHER MAN MORE THAN A YEAR AGO, WHY HAVE YOU CONSTANTLY PUT YOUR OWN LIFE IN JEOPARDY?

WHAT THE HELL ARE YOU *TALKING* ABOUT? I DON'T *ASK* FOR SHIT LIKE THIS TO HAPPEN TO ME, IT JUST--

HWUUUUHHHH

KOFF
KOFF
KOFF

ACCORDING TO AGENT 355'S JOURNALS, IN SEPTEMBER OF 2002, YOU DELIBERATELY REVEALED YOURSELF TO A GROUP OF GUN-TOTING REPUBLICAN WIDOWS.

WHY?

THAT WAS A... A COMPLICATED SITUATION. YOU DON'T--

GWUH!

STOP IT!

A FEW DAYS LATER, YOU CONFRONTED A PACK OF AMAZONS, SAYING SOMETHING TO THE EFFECT OF, "IF THIS IS YOUR WORLD, I WANT OUT. JUST GO AHEAD AND KILL ME ALREADY."

THAT'S... THAT'S TAKEN OUT OF CONTEXT.

HAVE IT YOUR WAY.

HAAAAAAA!

STOP... PLEASE...

WEEKS LATER, YOU UNNECESSARILY INVOLVED YOURSELF IN AN ALTERCATION WITH TWO ARMED VAGRANTS ON A TRAIN FROM--

SO WHAT?

CHRIST, HOW MANY OF MY GODDAMN GREATEST HITS DO WE HAVE TO GO OVER? WHAT'S THE POINT?

HAVE YOU EVER CONTEMPLATED TAKING YOUR OWN LIFE, YORICK?

BACK INTO THE DRINK THEN...

WAIT! JUST WAIT.

THE PLAGUE WAS 7/17, RIGHT?

THIS... THIS WAS THREE DAYS LATER. JULY TWENTIETH...

I HAD ONLY LEFT MY CRAPPY STUDIO APARTMENT ONCE SINCE THE SHIT HIT THE FAN, AND AS SOON AS I SAW WHAT WAS DOWN IN MY LOBBY, I...I WENT RIGHT BACK INSIDE.

IT'S NOT LIKE THERE WERE PLACES TO VOLUNTEER OR ANYONE TO GIVE BLOOD TO. IT WAS JUST THE END OF THE WORLD, THAT'S ALL.

YOU HAVE TO UNDERSTAND, I ONLY KNEW WHAT WAS GOING ON FROM WHAT I COULD HEAR ON THOSE LAST FEW RADIO BROADCASTS BEFORE THE BATTERIES IN MY WALKMAN RAN OUT.

I KNEW THAT ALL OF THE MEN WERE DEAD IN AT LEAST NEW YORK CITY, AND I KNEW I WOULD DIE PRETTY SOON, TOO.

I MEAN, OBVIOUSLY I WAS INFECTED WITH WHATEVER OFFED EVERYBODY ELSE, RIGHT?

WHY WOULD I BE ANY DIFFERENT?

BUT A FEW DAYS LATER, I STILL WASN'T DEAD, AND MY NEW PET AND I WERE DOWN TO TOILET WATER AND OLD CONDIMENT PACKS FOR RATIONS.

≥AW SEEK≤

SO I FINALLY DECIDED TO VENTURE OUTSIDE MY BUILDING.

221

APPARENTLY, SHE HAD GONE ALL HEDDA GABLER RIGHT AFTER THE PLAGUE HIT.

YOU KNOW HEDDA GABLER, RIGHT? IBSEN PLAY ABOUT A CHICK WHO SHOOTS HERSELF IN THE FACE?

BUT HEDDA SHOT HERSELF BECAUSE SHE COULDN'T ENDURE LIFE IN A PATRIARCHAL SOCIETY.

THIS COP JUST SAW THE PATRIARCHY *EVAPORATE*--SAW EVERY SEXIST PARTNER WHO EVER HIT ON HER AND EVERY SCUMMY CROOK WHO CALLED HER BITCH *DIE*-- AND SHE *STILL* KILLED HERSELF.

AND THEN I THOUGHT, IF SOME TOUGH BROAD FROM NEW YORK'S FINEST COULDN'T MAKE IT IN THIS WORLD, HOW AM *I* SUPPOSED TO?

I WAS STILL HAVING AN IMPOSSIBLE TIME COPING WITH THE TWIN TOWERS, HOW THE FUCK WAS I GONNA DEAL WITH *THIS?*

AND SUDDENLY, I FELT THIS...THIS INTENSE *JEALOUSY* FOR ALL THE OTHER GUYS AROUND ME. IT WAS LIKE, THEY HAD CROSSED THE FINISH LINE ALREADY, YOU KNOW? BUT I STILL HAD A MILLION LAPS TO RUN.

AND THEN I REMEMBERED THIS THING MY *GRANDFATHER* ONCE TOLD ME AND...

WHATEVER.

I KNEW I WAS DONE.

BUT YOU WEREN'T DONE.

NOT UNLESS I'M IN HELL NOW.

YOU REALIZED THAT YOU WERE STRONGER THAN SOME PATHETIC LITTLE METER MAID.

I... I GUESS SO.

BULLSHIT!

AHN!

KRACK!

THAT WOMAN HAD THE BALLS TO DO SOMETHING YOU COULD ONLY *DREAM* OF. YOU WERE TOO MUCH OF A *COWARD* TO PULL THAT TRIGGER.

NO! AT THE LAST SECOND, I...I CHANGED MY MIND!

I GRABBED A GAS MASK FROM THE COP'S SQUAD CAR, GOT AMPERSAND, AND... AND WENT TO FIND MY *FAMILY*, TO FIND *BETH*.

IS THAT WHY YOU LEFT?

OR DEEP DOWN, DID YOU KNOW THAT IF YOU THREW YOURSELF INTO ENOUGH DANGEROUS SITUATIONS, SOONER OR LATER...

SOMEONE WOULD PUT A HOLE IN YOUR HEAD *FOR* YOU?

THINK ABOUT IT.

AM I WRONG?

I SAW PART OF THIS PLAY ONCE, NOT IBSEN, A...A PLAY THAT SOME LADY IN NEBRASKA WROTE *AFTER* THE PLAGUE. A PLAY ABOUT THE LAST MAN ON EARTH.

AND SHE SAID THAT IT ENDED... THAT IT ENDED WITH THE LAST GUY KILLING HIM-SELF, "AND LETTING THE WOMEN SAVE THEM-SELVES."

AND AS SOON AS I HEARD THAT, I KNEW IT WAS THE PERFECT ENDING--I'VE *ALWAYS* KNOWN-- BUT I LASHED OUT, MADE FUN OF HER BECAUSE...

I KNOW WHAT I NEED TO DO, OKAY? BUT I CAN'T DO IT ALONE.

PLEASE.

IF THAT'S WHAT YOU REALLY WANT.

...DIE.

WHAT THE FUCK IS GOING ON?

THIS... THIS IS *YOUR* CABIN. YOU SAID--

I HAD TO SAY A *LOT* OF THINGS, YORICK. BUT YOU CAN RELAX NOW. IT'S OVER.

WHAT'S OVER?

WHAT THE *FUCK* IS OVER?

YOUR SUICIDE INTERVENTION.

MY **WHAT**?

IT'S CALLED LE PRÉCEDÉ D'ENFER, A FORM OF AVERSION THERAPY DEVELOPED DURING A SECRET MEETING BETWEEN BENJAMIN FRANKLIN AND THE MARQUIS DE SADE.

IT'S BASED ON THE IDEA THAT YOUR SEXUALITY AND MORTALITY ARE INDISSOLUBLE ELEMENTS OF--

WHAT... WHAT **ARE** YOU?

I'M AN AGENT OF THE CULPER RING. I HELP GET PEOPLE WHERE THEY NEED TO BE.

IT'S WHAT WE **DO**.

JESUS, DID...DID **355** KNOW ABOUT THIS?

IS THAT WHY SHE BROUGHT ME TO YOU?

NO, THIS WAS MY DECISION AND MY DECISION ALONE. AFTER RECOGNIZING YOUR SYMPTOMS IN 355'S JOURNALS, I FELT IT WAS NECESSARY TO TAKE DRASTIC MEASURES.

BUT IF 355 **DID** HAVE SOMETHING TO DO WITH THIS, WOULD...WOULD YOU TELL ME?

RIGHT.

BUT...HOW DID YOU *KNOW*? EVERYONE ELSE JUST THINKS I'M DUMB AND IMPULSIVE AND...WELL, NOT THAT I'M *NOT*, BUT HOW DID YOU KNOW THAT I--

LIFE IS MISERY, YORICK.

YOU'RE NOT THE ONLY ONE WHO EVER WANTED TO GET IT OVER WITH.

OH, WELL, I'M...I'M SORRY I HIT YOU AT THE END OF OUR, *um, SESSION.*

YORICK, I JAMMED A HYPO-DERMIC IN YOUR NECK AND CALLED YOU *FAGGOT.*

YOU HAVE NOTHING TO APOLOGIZE FOR.

BUT IT WAS *INCREDIBLE,* 711! THE LAST TIME I WENT UNDER, I SAW--

THE PROCESS IS BASED ON SECRECY, YORICK. ANY EPIPHANIES YOU MAY HAVE HAD DURING YOUR JOURNEY SHOULD BE KEPT TO YOURSELF.

BUT DON'T YOU WANT TO KNOW WHAT I SAW THAT...THAT MADE ME WANT TO *LIVE?*

NO.

BUT WHATEVER IT WAS, DON'T *FUCKING* FORGET IT.

231

355! DR. MANN!

WHERE'S AMPERSAND? IS...IS HE...?

HE'S *FINE*, YORICK.

ALTHOUGH THE ANTIBIOTICS MAKE HIS STOOL EXTREMELY SOFT, AS THE UNGRATEFUL LITTLE *FUCK* WILL BE HAPPY TO SHOW YOU.

YES!

YOU TWO FOUND A WAY INSIDE THE HOSPITAL?

EVENTUALLY, ALTHOUGH IT WAS A BIT MORE OF AN *EVENT* THAN I WOULD HAVE LIKED.

I WONDER IF ETHER-RAGGING A SECURITY GUARD IS A VIOLATION OF MY HIPPOCRATIC OATH?

HOW ABOUT YOU, YORICK? YOU DO ANYTHING *EXCITING?*

232

NOT UNLESS YOU CALL READING THREE HUNDRED PAGES OF *WAR AND PEACE* EXCITING.

≀MURN≀ MURN≀

HE DIDN'T CAUSE TOO MUCH TROUBLE, DID HE?

I HARDLY KNEW HE WAS HERE.

I CAN'T THANK YOU ENOUGH FOR THIS, 711. IF YOU WANT TO JOIN US FOR THE LAST LEG OF OUR TRIP TO SAN FRAN, I COULD USE A HAND WITH MY *OTHER* ASSIGNMENT AFTER I GET 'RICK TO--

I APPRECIATE IT, SWEETIE, BUT I HAVEN'T BEEN IN THE FIELD SINCE MY HUSBAND DIED. I'D JUST GET IN THE WAY.

THIS IS WHERE I BELONG NOW.

WELL, IT WAS GOOD TO HANG, 711.

THANKS FOR THE, UH, READING MATERIAL.

I THINK YOU'LL ENJOY IT, YORICK, AS LONG AS YOU'RE PATIENT. TRY NOT TO SKIP AHEAD, OKAY?

ENDINGS HAVE TO BE *EARNED.*

233

234

OH, NOT *YOU* FUCKS.

WHAT'S WITH THE GETUPS? THOSE SUPPOSED TO BE *IRONIC*?

SOMETHING LIKE THAT.

LISTEN, WE HAVE REASON TO BELIEVE THAT THE AMULET OF HELENE MAY HAVE PASSED THROUGH HERE ALREADY.

I HAVE NO IDEA WHAT YOU'RE--

KLICK

KLICK

KLICK

FINE.

I'VE GOT IT RIGHT HERE. JUST LET ME--

DON'T!

PAFT

PAFT

PAFT

Queensbrook, Arizona
Now

'COURSE.

NO DISRESPECT.

LEAH, YOU WANNA TELL US WHY YOU'RE HERE THIS EVENING, IN THE 227th YEAR OF THIS ONCE-GREAT NATION'S INDEPENDENCE?

UM, TO DEFEND THE LIBERTY OF THE CITIZENS OF THE STATE OF ARIZONA, THROUGH EDUCATION AND SERVICE.

YEP.

AND AS AN OFFICIAL MEMBER OF OUR BROTHERHOOD, WHO ELSE WILL YOU WELCOME TO APPLY FOR MEMBERSHIP?

ALL MEN AND WOMEN... WELL, JUST **WOMEN** NOW... OVER THE AGE OF SIXTEEN, REGARDLESS OF, UH... RACE OR CREED, SO LONG AS THEY SUPPORT OUR CONSTITUTION.

THAT'S MY DARLING.

LEAH, I WAS SAVING THIS FOR ONE OF YOUR **BROTHERS'** INDUCTIONS, BUT SINCE THEY'RE NO LONGER WITH US...

FOR SERIOUS?

YOU SWEAR TO ALWAYS DO WHAT'S RIGHT FOR YOUR BELOVED STATE?

HELL, YEAH.

EVEN IF...?

Fourteen Miles East
Six Hours Earlier

WHAT'S YOUR POISON, 355?

I DON'T KNOW. MAYBE THOSE THINGS THEY USED AT SCHOOL BEFORE PHOTOCOPIES... MIMEOGRAPHS?

I LIKED THE WAY THEY SMELLED WHEN THEY WERE WARM.

MIMEOGRAPHS?

WHEN WERE YOU A STUDENT, THE 1800'S?

I'M ONLY A FEW YEARS OLDER THAN YOU, ASSFACE.

HOW ABOUT YOU, DR. MANN?

PYGMY SHREWS.

YOU...LIKE THE SMELL OF PYGMY SHREWS?

I DON'T GIVE A FUCK ABOUT THE SMELL OF ANYTHING.

THE PYGMY SHREW JUST BECAME EXTINCT.

RIGHT THIS SECOND?

IT'S BEEN MORE THAN A YEAR AND A HALF SINCE THE PLAGUE KILLED EVERY MAMMAL WITH A PENIS EXCEPT FOR YOU AND AMPERSAND, CORRECT?

WELL, AS FAR AS WE--

THE PYGMY SHREW HAS A LIFESPAN OF A YEAR AND A HALF. WITH NOTHING LEFT TO GET KNOCKED UP BY, THAT MEANS THEY'RE GONE NOW. ALL OF THEM.

IN A FEW MONTHS OPOSSUMS WILL BE WIPED OUT, TOO.

HOW SERIOUS IS THAT, ALLISON?

HOW SERIOUS? IN THE GRAND SCHEME OF THINGS? WHO GIVES A SHIT?

BUT A FEW MONTHS AFTER THAT, THE LAST RATS WILL START TO DIE. AND AFTER THEY DIE--

DOGGIES!

YORICK, ARE YOU RETARDED? MOST CANINES LIVE--

NO, I MEAN... DOGGIES!

RRRRRRR

RRRRRR

RRRRRRR

243

JESUS FUCK.

DON'T BE SCARED, LITTLE--

KA-BLAM

HEY!

WAS THAT *NECESSARY?* THEY WERE MORE AFRAID OF *US* THAN--

YORICK, THOSE BONES WERE *HUMAN.*

WHAT...?

OVER HERE.

LOOKS LIKE THERE WERE ABOUT SIX OF THEM. MAYBE MORE, BUT THE BUZZARDS PROBABLY--

WHAT IS *WRONG* WITH PEOPLE?

THE HIGHWAYS ARE OPEN OUT HERE! I MEAN, IT WASN'T RUSH HOUR WHEN THE PLAGUE HIT *THIS* TIME ZONE. HOW MANY CARS HAVE DRIVEN PAST THESE GUYS SINCE THEN?

AND NOT *ONE* WOMAN CAN STOP AND... AND GIVE THEM A DECENT BURIAL?

I'M SORRY, 'RICK, BUT YOU KNOW THE STORY.

WHEN THREE BILLION PEOPLE DIE IN ONE DAY--

YO!

GET AWAY FROM THOSE BOYS!

ISN'T THIS THE PART WHERE YOU DO SOMETHING STUPID?

THAT WAS OLD YORICK.

NEW YORICK *AVOIDS* THE VIOLENT FEMMES.

WHAT ARE YOU TALKING ABOUT?

YOU CAME AT US WITH A *WEAPON.*

CAME AT YOU? I WAS OUT HUNTING *DINNER.* I HEARD A SHOT, SO I...I CAME RUNNING.

TO SAVE OUR LIVES?

YES! THE LOCAL MILITIA PSYCHOS HAVE RIGGED CORPSES WITH BOOBY TRAPS TO... TO SCARE AWAY "OUTSIDERS."

I DIDN'T WANT TO SEE SOME GOOD SAMARITAN GET HER HAND BLOWN OFF BY A CLAYMORE.

WHY SHOULD WE BELIEVE SOME SKINHEAD?

HEY, THIS IS *PRACTICAL,* NOT POLITICAL. IN CASE YOU HAVEN'T NOTICED, LONG LOCKS AND DESERT HEAT GO TOGETHER LIKE ORANGE JUICE AND COLGATE.

AND NOW THAT THE LESS-FAIR SEX HAS PASSED ON, OUR HAIR IS PRETTY MUCH...

... IS THAT A *DUDE?*

ME? UH, NO.

SEE, I HAVE REAL BAD ALLERGIES, SO--

OKAY, THAT IS THE **WORST** FAKE CHICK VOICE I HAVE EVER HEARD. AND LOOK AT YOUR HANDS! YOU'RE **TOTALLY** A DUDE!

MY COMPANION HAS A HORMONE CONDITION THAT MAKES HER LOOK AND SOUND--

OH, GIVE IT UP, AGENT 355. JUST TELL HER THE TRUTH. WHAT **DIFFERENCE** DOES IT MAKE?

HIDIGEY, IDIGALLIDIGISIDIGON! ZIDIGIP IDIGIT!

DIDIGONT YIDIGOU **TIDIGELL** MIDIGE WHIDIGAT TIDIGO DIDIGO!

DON'T MIND THEM. THEY DO THIS ALL THE TIME. I THINK IT'S **CHINESE**.

ALL RIGHT, NOW I **KNOW** YOU'RE A DUDE. THAT'S **GIBBERISH**, IT'S LIKE PIG LATIN ONLY GIRLS KNOW HOW TO SPEAK.

NEVER HEARD ANYBODY DO IT THAT FAST THOUGH.

OH, WHAT THE FUCK?

YOU GUYS TOLD ME THAT WAS CHINESE!

HOLY...

YOU...YOU *ARE* A MAN. I DIDN'T REALLY *BELIEVE*...

WHOOPSIE-DAISY.

FIDIGUCKIDIGING *HIDIGELL.*

YES, YORICK IS--IN THE LOOSEST SENSE OF THE WORD-- A *MAN.*

AND IF YOU TAKE US SOME-WHERE WHERE WE CAN SIT DOWN AND REFILL OUR CANTEENS, WE'LL TELL YOU THE WHOLE *UNBEARABLY TEDIOUS* STORY.

MY...MY GARAGE IS RIGHT UP THE ROAD.

JESUS, AM I DREAMING?

LADY, *DAVID LYNCH'S* DREAMS WEREN'T THIS WEIRD.

FRN ADK

P.J.'s GAS

Certified Welding and other crap

WOW, YOU REALLY KNOW WHAT TO DO WITH ALL THIS STUFF, P.J.?

WELL, **THAT'S** CONDESCENDING.

BUT YEAH, I FIGURE I'M PROBABLY THE ONLY PERSON STILL ALIVE WHO CAN FIX A WASSER-BOXER PANCAKE WITH A BROKEN STEEL TIMING BELT.

I WISH WE HAD YOU AROUND WHEN OUR PIECE OF SHIT MINIVAN BROKE DOWN OUTSIDE TUBA CITY.

TELL ME ABOUT IT. I'D PROBABLY BE A MILLIONAIRE BY NOW... IF THOSE **SONS OF ARIZONA** BITCHES HADN'T CHOKED TRAFFIC DOWN TO LESS THAN ZERO.

WHO?

SONS OF ARIZONA...WHICH WAS A PRETTY STUPID NAME FOR A MILITIA EVEN WHEN ALL THE MEN **WEREN'T** DEAD. THEY'RE THE SAME CHICKS WHO RIGGED THOSE DEAD GUYS TO BLOW.

THE S.O.A. THINK THE **FEDERAL GOVERNMENT** IS RESPONSIBLE FOR THE PLAGUE, SO IN SOME KIND OF FUCKED-UP PROTEST, THEY CUT INTERSTATE 40 IN TWO.

OH, CHRIST.

THE McVEIGH GAMBIT.

WITH SO FEW FEMALE FIREFIGHTERS AROUND, 355 THOUGHT IT WOULD BE SAFER TO DETOUR THROUGH ARIZONA THAN TO RISK A TRIP THROUGH MORMON HELLFIRE.

OUT OF THE FRYING PAN, HUH?

WELL, YOU CAN ALWAYS HAVE A TRUCK FROM MY FLEET, TAKE YOUR CHANCES WITH AN ALTERNATE ROUTE.

HOW MANY CHOICES DO WE HAVE LEFT? I-10? I-8?

WHAT IF RUBY RIDGE LUNATICS HAVE TAKEN *THOSE* ROADS HOSTAGE?

THEN WE'LL GO DOWN TO MEXICO AND COME UP THROUGH SAN DIEGO.

BULLSHIT! WE CAN'T AFFORD TO WASTE ANY MORE TIME, 355!

WHAT DO YOU WANT ME TO DO, ALLISON? DRAG YOU AND YORICK THROUGH A WARZONE?

ISN'T THAT WHAT YOU'VE BEEN DOING FOR THE LAST EIGHTEEN MONTHS? BESIDES, I THOUGHT YOUR LITTLE CLUB WAS *CREATED* TO DEAL WITH CRAP LIKE THIS!

THE REST OF THE CULPER RING AND I WILL WORK ON OPENING INTERSTATE 40...*AFTER* I GET YOU AND YORICK TO OUR FINAL DESTINATION.

WHEN WILL THAT BE, A *YEAR* FROM NOW?

BY THEN, SOME AMAZON WILL HAVE PROBABLY TORCHED *EVERYTHING* I USED TO MAKE MY DAUGHTER!

DAUGHTER?

DOC, YOU TOLD US THAT CLONE YOU GAVE BIRTH TO WAS A *BOY.*

AND THIS ISN'T THE FIRST TIME YOU'VE SUGGESTED OTHERWISE...

WHAT, AM I BEING **INTERROGATED** NOW? IT WAS A SLIP OF THE FUCKING TONGUE.

YOU'RE THE ONE WITH ALL THE SECRETS, 355! MAYBE THIS MILITIA IS RIGHT. MAYBE YOUR BOSSES **ARE** TO BLAME FOR THIS WHOLE GODDAMN NIGHTMARE.

ALLISON...

FORGET IT.

I NEED SOME AIR.

JEEZ, **PMS** MUCH?

I DIDN'T SAY IT.

I'M SORRY ABOUT THAT... AND I'M SORRY ABOUT BEFORE, P.J. THIS TRIP HASN'T BEEN EASY ON ANY OF US.

HEY, WATER UNDER THE WHATEVER. YOU GUYS ARE STILL WELCOME TO BUNK HERE TONIGHT, FIGURE OUT YOUR NEXT MOVE TOMORROW.

IT'S LIKE MY OLD MAN USED TO SAY...

...EVERYTHING LOOKS BETTER AFTER A GOOD NIGHT'S SLEEP.

BETH!

USE YOUR MAGIC, YORICK!

KILL THEM!

I...I CAN'T!

THEN RUN AWAY! BEFORE IT COMES!

IT CAN *SMELL* ME! IT CAN--

SNFF

XXXXXXXXX

YORICK!

YORICK, GET UP!

IS DR. MANN WITH YOU?

WHA?

NO, WHY WOULD SHE--

SHE'S MISSING!

ONE MINUTE SHE WAS SLEEPING ACROSS FROM ME, AND THE NEXT SHE'S *GONE.*

GONE WHERE? DID *SINEAD* DO SOMETHING TO--

I'M RIGHT HERE, DICK.

AND I DIDN'T HEAR HER LEAVE EITHER. ALL OF MY VEHICLES ARE STILL AROUND, TOO.

WELL, THAT'S GOOD.

I MEAN, SHE PROBABLY JUST WENT FOR A MIDNIGHT STROLL OR SOMETHING... *RIGHT?*

MOM! INCOMING!

I GOT HER, LEAH!

STATE YOUR BUSINESS OR DIE, WOMAN!

RELAX, I COME IN PEACE!

WHAT THE *HELL* DO YOU WANT?

Queensbrook, Arizona
Now

WELL, *THAT'S* GOING TO END BADLY.

COME ON, THIS IS IMPORTANT.

I TOLD YOU, 355, I HAVE NO IDEA *WHERE* DR. MANN WENT!

I KNOW, BUT I'M AFRAID I DO.

WHAT DOES *THAT* MEAN?

IT MEANS I HAVE TO GO AFTER HER, BEFORE SHE DOES SOMETHING SHE'LL REGRET.

YOU'RE *LEAVING?* BUT THE LAST TIME YOU PAWNED ME OFF TO SOME WOMAN, IT WAS... *STRANGE.*

AND THAT WAS ONE OF YOUR *FRIENDS!* WE'VE ONLY KNOWN KOJACK BACK THERE FOR A FEW HOURS!

'RICK, IF P.J. WANTED TO HURT YOU, SHE WOULD HAVE DONE IT ALREADY.

BUT JUST IN CASE, I'M LEAVING YOU WITH *THIS.*

OH MY GOD. I'VE FINALLY DRIVEN YOU INSANE.

LISTEN, THIS IS A WALTHER PPK. IT'S SMALL, BUT--

"--IT'S GOT A DELIVERY LIKE A BRICK THROUGH A PLATE GLASS WINDOW?"

YOU'VE SHOT ONE BEFORE?

NO, I'VE SEEN DR. NO.

JESUS, WHAT KIND OF SECRET AGENT DOESN'T KNOW JAMES BOND?

IT'S EASY TO FIRE, JUST POINT AND CLICK. GOD FORBID ANYTHING HAPPENS, YOU'LL WANT TO GO FOR CENTER MASS, NO TRICKY HEAD SHOTS OR--

YOU'RE SERIOUS?

BELIEVE ME, IF I HAD ANOTHER OPTION, I WOULD TAKE IT. BESIDES, IF EVERYTHING GOES ACCORDING TO PLAN, YOU'LL NEVER EVEN HAVE TO DRAW IT.

YEAH, GOOD THING OUR SHIT ALWAYS GOES ACCORDING TO PLAN...

MY NAME IS ALLISON MANN.

I'M A **DOCTOR.**

WELL, THAT ACCENT ISN'T LOCAL.

NO, I'M FROM... ALL OVER, REALLY.

YOU AN ABORTIONIST?

SAVE IT, ANGELENE. LEAH, CHECK HER OUT?

SURE THING, MOM.

I'M JOY. WHAT BUSINESS YOU GOT WITH THE **SONS OF ARIZONA,** DOCTOR?

TWO OF MY FRIENDS AND I ARE TRYING TO GET TO CALIFORNIA.

IT'S A MEDICAL EMERGENCY, SO I WAS HOPING YOU PEOPLE WOULD BE KIND ENOUGH TO LET US THROUGH YOUR... **OBSTRUCTION.**

SORRY, BILLY GOAT GRUFF.

NOBODY CROSSES FOR FREE.

ACTUALLY, I WAS HOPING I COULD **BARTER** FOR OUR SAFE PASSAGE.

DOC, THIS IS A POLITICAL REVOLUTION, NOT A **TOLLBOOTH.**

BESIDES, BEHIND ME IS THE MOST WELL-STOCKED COMPOUND IN THE **HEMISPHERE.** WHAT COULD **YOU** POSSIBLY HAVE THAT WE MIGHT NEED?

THE MECHANIC UP THE ROAD SAID THAT TWO OF YOUR GIRLS WERE RECENTLY **WOUNDED** IN A FIREFIGHT.

I'D LIKE TO OFFER THEM MY MEDICAL EXPERTISE.

WOMAN, THE "GIRLS" YOU'RE REFERRING TO WERE SOLDIERS OF VALOR. AND I SAY "WERE" BECAUSE BOTH OF THEM **PASSED ON** LAST NIGHT.

I'M...VERY SORRY.

I WISH I HAD MADE IT HERE SOONER.

AND WHAT THE HELL DIFFERENCE WOULD THAT'VE MADE?

WHAT DID YOU THINK? THAT EVERYONE OUT HERE IS SOME BACK-WARDS HICK? THAT WE DON'T KNOW HOW TO DRESS A **GSW?** GIVE A BLOOD TRANSFUSION?

I WAS A NURSE MANAGER IN AN **ER** FOR NINE **DAMN** YEARS, YOU CONDESCENDING PIECE OF **SHIT!**

I DIDN'T MEAN--

KRACK

266

SEE THAT, DARLING? KNOCKING SOMEONE OUT--EVEN A CIVVIE--ISN'T NEARLY AS SIMPLE AS IT LOOKS ON THE TV.

AHHHHHN!

DEFINITELY.

KRACK

WHY DOESN'T SHE JUST PLAY POSSUM?

SURVIVAL INSTINCT'S A BITCH THAT WAY. BRAIN WANTS YOUR BODY TO STAY UP, KEEP FIGHTIN' LONG AS IT CAN.

FUHH

HERE.

YOU GIVE HER A TRY.

ANYWAY, WHAT'S UP FOR YOU AFTER CALI?

IF 355 WILL LET ME, I'D LIKE TO GO TO AUSTRALIA, FIND MY GIRLFRIEND BETH.

AWW, THAT'S ROMANTIC... AND KIND OF *STUPID*.

IT'S THE DUAL NATURE OF MY CHARM.

HOW ABOUT YOU, P.J.? YOU CAN'T STAY IN MILITIA-VILLE FOREVER.

BULL*SHIT!* I'M NOT GONNA LET SOME SKANKS WHO'VE SEEN *RED DAWN* ONE TIME TOO MANY SCARE ME OFF. I WAS BORN AND RAISED HERE, AND THIS IS WHERE I'M GONNA KICK.

YOU WERE RAISED IN A *GARAGE?*

UP UNTIL I WAS SIXTEEN. THEN MY OLD MAN WANTED ME TO START *WORKING* FOR HIM, SO I RAN AWAY TO L.A., JOINED A CRAPPY SKA BAND.

I NEVER KNEW HOW MUCH I FUCKING LOVED CARS UNTIL I WAS SURROUNDED BY PEOPLE WHO DIDN'T KNOW JACK ABOUT 'EM.

EVERYONE WAS *WAY* MORE IMPRESSED THAT I COULD CHANGE THEIR OIL THAN THE FACT THAT I COULD HALF-WAY PLAY BASS...SO I CAME BACK.

I USED TO THINK DAD WAS TRYING TO KEEP ME DOWN BY MAKING ME GET INTO THE FAMILY BUSINESS, BUT I REALIZE IT WAS SORTA *EMPOWERING,* YOU KNOW?

A GUY TEACHING HIS ONLY *DAUGHTER* TO BE A GREASE MONKEY? FUCK, I HOPE I'M THAT BADASS WHEN I HAVE KIDS.

YOU... WANT TO HAVE *CHILDREN?*

NOT WITH *YOU,* SPAZ.

THEN... *HOW?*

I DON'T KNOW. IF YOU AND YOUR FRIENDS DON'T FIND A WAY, *SOME-BODY* WILL.

IT'S NOT LIKE WE'RE JUST GONNA BECOME *EXTINCT.*

SAID THE T-REX TO THE TRICERATOPS.

DINOSAURS DIDN'T REALLY *DIE,* YORICK. THEY JUST EVOLVED INTO SOMETHING NEW.

THAT'S PROBABLY WHAT'LL HAPPEN TO WOMEN. WE'LL ALL TURN INTO *BIRDS* OR WHATEVER.

WELL, YOUR OPTIMISM IS REFRESHING... AND KIND OF *STUPID.*

TO BIRDS OF A FEATHER THEN.

FROM MY PRIVATE STOCK. THEY'RE HOTTER THAN HELL SINCE I SAVE MY GENERATORS FOR THE *LIGHTS,* BUT I DON'T THINK THEY'VE SKUNKED YET.

OH, NO THANKS, P.J. I HAVE THE TOLERANCE OF A THIRD-GRADER. AND THE LAST TIME I GOT DRUNK, I STARTED SINGING IN *SPANISH* AND--

ICE COLD

COME ON, STRAIGHT EDGE.

HOW BAD CAN *ONE* BREW BE?

WHAT'S THE SITUATION IN THERE, MOM?

I'M LETTING ANGELENE PLAY BAD COP FOR A SPELL.

THAT DOCTOR'S HIDING SOMETHING, ALL RIGHT. I JUST CAN'T TELL *WHAT*.

YOU THINK TEXAS SENT HER? AS A SCOUT FOR MORE RANGERS OR SOMETHING?

EITHER THAT, OR THE SHADOW GOVERNMENT IS FINALLY MOVING INTO *PHASE TWO*.

I FIGURED IT WOULD TAKE ABOUT THIS LONG FOR CONDIE TO GET HER STORMTROOPERS OUT HERE.

LEAH, WHY DON'T YOU TAKE MY FORTY-SEVEN AND RUN SOME RECON ON P.J.'S?

I'VE LET THAT HAIRLESS DESERT RAT HOLD HER GROUND 'CAUSE HER DADDY WAS OKAY PEOPLE, BUT IF SHE'S HARBORING *FEDS*, OUR TRUCE IS OVER.

MAN, I WAS HOPING I COULD HELP INTERROGATE THE P.O.W.

DON'T WORRY, BABY.

IT'S NOT LIKE SHE'S *GOING* ANY-WHERE...

IF YOU DON'T WANNA GET SMACKED AGAIN, JUST ANSWER THE QUESTION.

HOW DID YOU KILL ALL THE MEN?

WAS IT A SATELLITE OR THE MEASLES VACCINATIONS? OR THOSE LITTLE ROBOTS IN THE BLOOD... *NANITES,* RIGHT?

JOY THINKS MAYBE THE U.N. HID SOMETHING IN ALL THE *PORNO,* BUT I KNOW THAT AIN'T IT. MY ERNIE NEVER WATCHED A'ONE OF THOSE IN HIS FORTY YEARS.

FUNNY SEEING YOU HERE.

SAY WHAT?

DOCTOR, CAN WE MAYBE SAVE THE DRAMATIC CONFESSIONS UNTIL WE'RE OUT OF THE KILL ZONE?

I DIDN'T BRING THE *BOY* ALONG, SO THESE CUFFS ARE GOING TO TAKE SOME--

355, BACK IN BOSTON, I LIED TO YOU ABOUT MY *BABY.*

I TOLD YOU THAT I'D *CLONED* MY *NEPHEW* BECAUSE WE COULDN'T FIND A TRANSPLANT DOCTOR OR SOME BULLSHIT...BUT I DON'T EVEN *HAVE* A NEPHEW. THAT WAS JUST A SOB STORY I *MADE UP.*

WHY?

I WAS SCARED. I...I THOUGHT THE GOVERNMENT HAD SENT YOU TO *ARREST* ME. I FIGURED YOU'D SHOW SOME MERCY IF MY EXPERIMENTS SOUNDED ALTRUISTIC.

SO WAIT, YOU *NEVER* GAVE BIRTH TO A CLONE?

OH, I DID...BUT IT WASN'T A BOY. IT WAS *ME.* I WAS PREGNANT WITH A CLONE OF *MYSELF.*

AT LEAST, THAT'S WHAT SHE WAS *SUPPOSED* TO BE. WHAT CAME OUT OF MY WOMB...IT WAS JUST A MESS OF LIMBS...AND *ORGANS* AND--

ALLISON...

NO, YOU DON'T UNDERSTAND. HER CONCEPTION WAS TOTALLY SELFISH AND...AND *IRRESPONSIBLE.*

BACK IN JAPAN, MY ASSHOLE FATHER WAS CLOSE TO CLONING *HIMSELF,* AND I WANTED TO SUCCEED BEFORE HE DID. WHO EVEN KNOWS IF HE EVER--

DOCTOR, WITH ALL DUE RESPECT, WHAT DOES THE SEX OF YOUR DEAD CHILD MATTER *NOW?*

DON'T YOU *GET* IT?

IT MATTERS BECAUSE IT MEANS I'M A FUCKING *FAILURE!*

COMPARED TO A BIOENGINEER LIKE MY DAD, I'M SLOW AND...AND *INCOMPETENT*. THE PLAGUE DIDN'T KILL MY BABY, MY SHODDY SCIENCE DID!

EVEN IF *I DO* FIGURE OUT WHAT CAUSED ALL THE MEN TO DIE, IT MIGHT TAKE ME *YEARS* TO SUCCESSFULLY CLONE A HUMAN BEING! YEARS THE WORLD DOESN'T HAVE!

YOU'RE IN *SHOCK*, DOCTOR. JUST TRY TO--

WE DON'T HAVE TIME, 355! WE DON'T HAVE TIME FOR MORE DETOURS AND...AND *SIDE TRIPS!* IT'S IMPERATIVE THAT I GET TO MY LAB AND START WORKING *NOW.*

THAT'S WHY I RISKED MY *LIFE* TO CUT THROUGH THIS--

ANGELENE?

...WHO THE HOLY HELL ARE *YOU?*

IF YOU MAKE ANOTHER SOUND, I WILL EMPTY THIS CLIP THROUGH YOUR *MOUTH.*

THAT .45 OF YOURS...IT'S *GOVERNMENT* ISSUE.

I WAS *RIGHT.*

GIVE ME THE KEYS TO HER HANDCUFFS.

NOW.

YOU LOOK GOOD WITH A GUN, FED, BUT YOU AIN'T A *KILLER*.

KLIK

OH, YOU'VE KILLED BEFORE. ANYONE CAN SEE THAT. BUT JUST 'CAUSE YOU DANCE DON'T MEAN YOU'RE A *DANCER*.

YOU FOLKS DON'T KNOW WHAT IT FEELS LIKE TO PULL A TRIGGER FOR YOUR HOME, FOR YOUR *FAMILY*. THAT'S WHY YOU'RE SO SLOW.

THAT'S WHY YOU'RE NOT GONNA SHOOT *ME*.

HELLLLP!

BITCH!

JUST LEAVE ME! TAKE YORICK AND--

SHUT UP!

THINK

WHAT THE FUCK IS--

HAA!

MY *EYEEEEE!*

OOF!

NEXT WOMAN INSIDE THIS TENT IS *DEAD!*

HEY, *FED.*

LITTLE TIP. YOU NEED A LOT MORE THAN ONE HIT TO KNOCK SOMEONE OUT...JUST ASK YOUR *GIRLFRIEND.*

NOW DROP YOUR TOYS, OR I TAKE HER FASTER THAN YOU WHORES TOOK MY *SONS.*

♪ RIIIIICO... ♪
SUAAAVEEE!

YOU HAVE THE WORST VOICE I HAVE EVER, EVER, **EVER** HEARD.

DEAL WITH IT, SWEET-HEART.

I'M THE ONLY **TENOR** THE PLANET'S GOT LEFT.

YOU'RE SO FULL OF SHIT.

NO, S'TRUE! OKAY, THERE MIGHT BE, LIKE, **FOUR** OLD LADIES WITH VOICES DEEPER THAN MINE, BUT--

NO, I MEAN YOU'RE FULL OF SHIT ABOUT **SEX.**

GAH, NOT **THIS** AGAIN...

SERIOUSLY, YOU'VE BEEN THE LAST COCK ON EARTH FOR **AGES.** HOW DO YOU NOT BONE **ONE** GIRL IN THAT WHOLE TIME?

AND SPANKING THE MONKEY'S **ENOUGH?**

THE WAY METHADONE IS ENOUGH FOR A HEROIN ADDICT, I GUESS.

AND **PLEASE** DON'T BRING MONKEYS INTO THIS...

HOW MANY TIMES?

IN A DAY? WELL, THERE WAS ONE PARTICULARLY TRYING INCIDENT DURING THE **CHICAGO** LEG OF OUR TRIP, AFTER WE STOPPED BY THESE OUTDOOR SHOWERS THE CITY HAD SET UP.

BY THE TIME I WAS DONE WITH THAT NIGHT'S SESSION, I WAS SO SPENT I THINK **BONE MARROW** STARTED COMING OUT.

I KNOW I SOUND REPRESSED, BUT I'M NOT SURE I COULD LIVE WITH THE ALTERNATIVE. PREYING ON LONELY WOMEN'S...**DESPERATION**, YOU KNOW?

HUH. I CAN RESPECT THAT, ACTUALLY. I MEAN, NO OFFENSE, BUT YOU'RE NOT EXACTLY THE KINDA GUY I WOULDA FUCKED **BEFORE** THE PLAGUE, SO I WOULDN'T FEEL RIGHT FUCKING YOU **NOW**.

THAT WOULD SORTA DEGRADE US BOTH.

THAT IS THE NICEST THING ANYONE HAS EVER SAID TO ME.

CHEERS, BIG EARS.

DOWN THE HATCH, TIGHT--

RARF RARF RARF RARF RARF RARF RARF

RARF
RARF RARF
RARF
RARF

WHAT THE HELL IS THAT ALL ABOUT?

SOUNDS LIKE THOSE WILD DOGS.

NO KIDDING, RETARD. WHY ARE THEY GOING *NUTS?*

MAYBE IT'S JUST 355 AND... AND DR. MANN COMING BACK.

AND MAYBE IT'S NOT.

P.J., DON'T!

I JUST REMEMBERED, I HAD THIS...THIS CRAZY VIVID *NIGHTMARE.* ABOUT SOMETHING *AWFUL* COMING. IF YOU GO OUT THERE--

YORICK, YOU'RE *SMASHED.* GO HIDE UNDER A DESK OR SOMETHING. I'LL BE RIGHT BACK.

BUT...

ARR FARR

I KNOW, ALL RIGHT! I'M NOT GOING TO *USE* IT, I JUST--

HEY!

Queensbrook, Arizona
Now

OH.

OH, FUCK.

THAT... THAT WAS *YOUR* FAULT, BITCH! THAT SHIT IS ON *YOU!*

I DIDN'T WANT TO *SHOOT* YOUR ASS!

GODDAMN.

GODDAMN GREASE MONKEY MADE ME--

EEEE

THE HELL...?

LISTEN, I ALREADY SENT MY DAUGHTER TO SCOUT FOR THE REST OF YOUR CREW.

IF SHE COMES BACK AND TELLS US YOU LIED ABOUT *OTHER* FEDS HERE, I'M GOING TO HAVE TO TAKE THIS TO THOSE BIG BROWN *EYES* OF YOURS.

I TOLD YOU, I AM *NOT* A FEDERAL AGENT. DR. MANN AND I ARE *PHYSICIANS*, ON A HUMANITARIAN MISSION.

OH, YEAH? THEN I'M SURE YOU COULD ANSWER A QUESTION FROM MY FIRST-YEAR *NURSING EXAM.*

LIKE, LET'S SAY A PATIENT'S SUPPOSED TO GET 1,000 ML OF LACTATED BRINGER'S SOLUTION IN A FIVE-SHIFT. WHAT'S THE INFUSION RATE?

...

200 MILLILITERS AN HOUR.

AND IT'S *RINGER'S* SOLUTION, NOT BRINGER'S.

288

SHE'S *LYING*, JOY. WHY WOULD AN M.D. BE PACKING HARDWARE LIKE *THIS*?

GIRL'S *GOTTA* BE WORKING FOR THE SCUMBAGS WHO MADE WHATEVER KILLED OUR BOYS.

THE PLAGUE *ISN'T* MANMADE. IT *CAN'T* BE. WHO WOULD *GAIN* FROM KILLING ALL THE MEN?

OH, NOT *ALL* OF THEM. I'M SURE BUSH AND CHENEY AND ASHCROFT ARE STILL ALIVE IN MOUNT WEATHER, WAITING TO RELEASE THEIR *SHOCK TROOPS* ON US.

BUT THE SONS OF ARIZONA AIN'T GONNA GO OUT LIKE THE 50,000 GIRLS RAPED IN YUGOSLAVIA, OR THE 100,000 "COMFORT WOMEN" KIDNAPPED BY THE JAPS DURING--

GOD, STOP REGURGITATING WHATEVER *PROPAGANDA* YOUR HUSBANDS FED YOU! THERE *IS* NO WAR! ALL THIS BLOCKADE OF YOURS IS DOING IS *STARVING* THE COUNTRY!

AND WE'LL CONTINUE TO STARVE IT UNTIL AMERICA'S *FEVER* BREAKS... AND THE INFECTION OF GOVERNMENT HAS *PASSED*.

UHF!

KLANG

"200 MILLILITERS AN HOUR"?

NOT BAD, 355.

289

WHAT, I GOT IT RIGHT?

YOU WERE *BLUFFING?*

EDUCATED GUESS. MY MOM USED TO BE AN RN.

SHE'D LET ME MAKE THE ROUNDS WITH HER SOMETIMES. MY TOTAL RECALL STRETCHES BACK PRETTY FAR, BUT I WASN'T SURE IF--

YOU...YOU *NEVER* TALK ABOUT YOUR FAMILY, 355. I DIDN'T KNOW YOUR MOTHER'S IN *MEDICINE.*

SHE WAS. DIED WHEN I WAS EIGHT. WITH MY DAD AND MY BABY SISTER.

CAR ACCIDENT.

I'M...I'M SORRY.

I'M SO SORRY...

I'M NOT ASKING YOU AGAIN, LADY.

WHO THE **HELL** ARE YOU TALKING TO?

I'M NOT A LADY.

AND I'M TALKING TO MY **MONKEY**.

BUT HE'S **JUST** A MONKEY. HE DOESN'T UNDERSTAND ME. AND THAT'S **MY** FAULT. I... I DIDN'T TRAIN HIM WELL ENOUGH.

HOLY FUCKING...

YOU'RE A...A...

MAN, I'M NOT EVEN *DRUNK* ANYMORE.

I'VE NEVER *BEEN* SO SOBER. I MEAN, THIS MUST BE THE *DEFINITION* OF SOBER.

CAN I ASK HOW OLD YOU ARE?

YOU SEEM A LITTLE YOUNG TO BE A *MURDERER.*

NO...THAT CHICK DREW ON *ME!* I *HAD* TO!

SHE WASN'T A "CHICK."

HER NAME WAS P.J. SHE PLAYED THE BASS AND FIXED CARS AND--

SHUT UP, ALREADY!

YEAH, YOU SOUND LIKE MY SISTER.

SHE KILLED AN INNOCENT WOMAN, TOO.

RAAK

293

WE SHOULD TALK, 355.

IN A SECOND, DOCTOR. P.J. SAID THERE WERE ONLY EIGHT WOMEN IN THIS CAMP, RIGHT?

WITH JOY'S KID ON PATROL AND TWO OF HER SOLDIERS IN THE MORGUE, THAT LEAVES JUST *FIVE* PEOPLE OUT THERE. IF I CAN TIME THINGS EXACTLY RIGHT--

355, AREN'T YOU WONDERING WHY I *KEPT* LYING TO YOU ABOUT CLONING MY "SICK NEPHEW"? EVEN *AFTER* I KNEW YOU HAD NO INTENTION OF ARRESTING ME FOR MY EXPERIMENTS?

IT'S BECAUSE I DIDN'T WANT YOU TO THINK I WAS SOME KIND OF *MAD SCIENTIST.* I KNOW IT'S JUVENILE, BUT I...I WANTED YOU TO *LIKE* ME.

I *DO* LIKE YOU, ALISON.

HOLD ON.

YOU MEAN...*LIKE* YOU LIKE YOU?

JESUS, YOU'RE EVEN STARTING TO *TALK* LIKE YORICK.

I MEAN, I'VE ALWAYS KNOWN YOU WERE...*YOU KNOW,* BUT I NEVER THOUGHT YOU HAD ANY INTEREST IN--

YOU TWO STILL PLAYING DOCTOR?

DON'T WORRY, THEY'RE NOT EXACTLY *MARKSMEN,* BUT THEY SHOULD MAKE THIS RELATIVELY *QUICK.*

ANY FINAL WORDS, FED?

YEAH, DIDIGO IDIGANY IDIGOF YIDIGOU SPIDIGEAK GIDIGIBBIDIGER-IDIGISH?

WHAT THE HELL IS *THAT* SUPPOSED TO MEAN?

IDIGAL-LIGISADIGON. PRIDIGETIDIGEND TIDIGO BIDIGE *SIDIGICK,* IDIGAND DRIDIGOP TIDIGO IDIGALL FIDIGOURS.

SPEAK *ENGLISH* YOU SON OF A--

RIDIGIGHT...

HEY, DON'T YOU *DARE* PUKE ON MY--

UNF!

Three Hours Later

YORICK, WHAT *HAPPENED?*

355. DOC.

ARE... ARE YOU GUYS *OKAY?*

WHAT *IS* THIS, 'RICK?

WHERE'S P.J.?

SHE WAS *ATTACKED.* BY ONE OF THE GIRLS FROM THAT MILITIA. THEY... THEY ENDED UP *SHOOTING* EACH OTHER.

I WANTED TO DO SOMETHING, BUT...BUT AMPERSAND *LOST* THE GUN YOU GAVE ME, SO ALL WE COULD DO IS HIDE.

I'M SUCH A COWARD, I--

DON'T BE RIDICULOUS, YORICK.

YOU DID THE RIGHT THING.

WHAT ABOUT YOU TWO?

WHERE *WERE* YOU?

WE'LL TELL YOU ON THE WAY TO DR. MANN'S BACK-UP LAB IN SAN FRAN. I DON'T WANT TO SPEND ANOTHER SECOND OUT HERE.

BUT THE *ROADBLOCK*...

IT'S *UNBLOCKED.*

P.J. DIDN'T GIVE HER LIFE IN VAIN. MILLIONS OF PEOPLE WILL BE ABLE TO GET PROVISIONS NOW THAT I-40 IS OPEN AGAIN.

CHRIST, HOW MANY MORE WOMEN HAVE TO *DIE* BEFORE WE CAN *SAVE* THEM?

I CAN'T APOLOGIZE ENOUGH, YORICK.

THIS ALL STARTED BECAUSE I DIDN'T TELL YOU AND 355 THE *TRUTH.* BUT I PROMISE, FROM HERE ON OUT...

...NO MORE LIES.

Oldenbrook, Kansas
Now

THE ASTRONAUT WOMAN?

BUT HER CHILD TODDLER--

--CAME A FEW DAYS EARLIER THAN EXPECTED.

ONE SECOND, DR. WEBER WAS GOING INTO LABOR, AND THE NEXT, THE BABY WAS *CROWNING!* I'VE NEVER SEEN SUCH AN EFFORTLESS--

Y? Y? Y? AND? AND? AND?

AND EVERYTHING'S FINE.

HER *SON* IS FINE.

ALIVE?! A MALE WITH ACTUAL BREATH IS PASSING THROUGH THE VAGINA!

SPASIBO, IISUS HRISTOS! SLAVA BOGU!

UM. RIGHT!

BUT WE'LL HAVE TO KEEP THE BOY DOWNSTAIRS IN THE HOT SUITE UNTIL WE'RE *CERTAIN* THAT THE ENVIRONMENT POSES NO THREAT TO HIM. MY SISTER AND I THINK--

PARDON ME.

"Safeword, Chapter One"
The Full Script for Y #18
Prepared for Vertigo Comics,
June 30, 2003
Brian K. Vaughan

Page One

Page One, Panel One
We open with this close-up of YORICK BROWN, age *eight* (or so). It's 1989. He has braces and a stupid haircut, but he's still our Yorick.

1) <u>Someone's Voice (from off)</u>: Yorick *always* gets to be last!

Page One, Panel Two
White text, black background, etc.

2) <u>White text on black background</u>:
Cleveland, Ohio
Fifteen Years Ago

Page One, Panel Three
Pull out for this largest panel of the page, at least a half-SPLASH. We can now see that we're inside of a "retirement home." ELDERLY WOMEN are shuffling along, playing bridge in the background, etc., but there should be no elderly *males* in this shot. Standing outside of a doorway to one of the nursing facility rooms are Yorick, HERO, and their father, PROFESSOR BROWN (the bearded guy we saw in a photo back in Issue #11, I think). Hero is twelve or eleven here, and she's throwing a little fit. Prof. Brown is trying to calm her down. Watching this confrontation with interest is Yorick, who we can now see is wearing an over-sized purple T-shirt with a picture of Jack Nicholson as the Joker on the front of it. *(Will, please give us a heads-up now if that will be a problem with legal or anything. This is actually an important bit of costuming, since this story is about "Yorick the Jester" in a lot of ways.)*

3) <u>Hero</u>: How come *he* can't go in first?

4) <u>Prof. Brown</u>: Hero, I'm not asking you to charge into battle against King Charles' cavalry.

5) <u>Prof. Brown</u>: I just want you to say hello to your *grandfather*.

Page Two

Page Two, Panel One
Push in closer on the Professor and his daughter, who almost looks frightened here.

    1) <u>Prof. Brown</u>: You know he gets confused if we all try to talk with him at the same—

    2) <u>Hero</u>: I don't care!
    3) <u>Hero</u>: I... I don't even *like* him! He always tries to touch my—

Page Two, Panel Two
Cut over to Yorick, nobly volunteering.

    4) <u>Yorick</u>: It's okay, Dad.
    5) <u>Yorick</u>: I can go in first.

Page Two, Panel Three
This largest panel of the page can be from Hero's point-of-view. The Professor affectionately musses Yorick's hair as he addresses his off-panel daughter. Now that his father isn't looking, Yorick crosses his eyes and sticks out his tongue at the off-panel Hero.

    6) <u>Prof. Brown</u>: There's a brave soldier.
    7) <u>Prof. Brown</u>: He didn't even need a St. Crispin's Day speech to get *him* onto the front line.

Page Two, Panel Four
This is just a shot of the pissed-off young Hero, crossing her arms and muttering under her breath.

    8) <u>Hero (small, under her breath)</u>: I hope you both get *AIDS*.

Page Two, Panel Five
We're behind Yorick here, cheated so we can see some of his expression, as he knocks on the frame of the open door. Inside this room, we can see an elderly man in the background. He's seated with his back to us, and we can't see his face. He's apparently staring out the window. This shot should be creepy and ominous, Pia.

    9) <u>Yorick</u>: Hello?
    10) <u>Yorick</u>: Grampy... ?

Page Three

Page Three, Panel One
Change angles for this largest panel of the page. We're now in the foreground with Yorick's gruff, eighty-year-old GRANDFATHER (a man that Yorick will look almost identical to when we see *him* at this age... oops, did I give something away?). In the background, Yorick cautiously steps into the dimly lit room.

    1) <u>Yorick</u>: It's me.
    2) <u>Yorick</u>: Yorick.

    3) <u>Grandpa</u>: Yorick *who*?

Page Three, Panel Two
Push in closer on the two, as "Grampy" smiles and turns to greet his smirking grandchild.

    4) <u>Yorick</u>: Ha ha, hilarious.

    5) <u>Grandpa</u>: Come here, ya little bastard. What brings you to this dump?

    6) <u>Yorick</u>: Mom's in town for campaign stuff, remember?

Page Three, Panel Three

Change angles, as a curious Yorick interrogates his surly elder. Please leave some room between them for this exchange:

7) Yorick: Hey, how come there are so many women in here?

8) Grandpa: 'Cause women live longer than men.

9) Yorick: Why?

10) Grandpa: 'Cause they suck all the goddamn life out of us.

Page Three, Panel Four

Similar framing, but now Yorick's frail grandfather becomes fairly irate.

11) Yorick: Oh.
12) Yorick: Well, it must be cool to be, like, the only guy with so many girls all over the place.

13) Grandpa: You *crazy*? It's hell on earth! Ain't nothing worse than ladies in numbers.

Page Three, Panel Five

And we end with this portentous close-up of Yorick's grandfather, as he warns:

14) Grandpa: Someday, you'll understand...

Page Four

Page Four, Panel One

Cut to the present day for this close-up of a clean-shaven ADULT YORICK. He has the hood of his dark blue poncho up, but no gas mask on. He's screaming at the top of his lungs.

1) Yorick: AHHHHH!

Page Four, Panel Two

What's black and white and a recurring panel gimmick that this writer seemingly never tires of?

2) White text on black background:

Allenspark, Colorado
Now

Page Four, Panel Three

Pull out to the largest panel of the page, at least a half-SPLASH. We're in the foreground with the still-screaming Yorick, who we can now see is sitting behind AGENT 355 on a large two-passenger ATV. Tied to the front of this speeding all-terrain vehicle is a pet carrier, which we will eventually learn houses a sickly Ampersand.

More importantly, we can see that 355 and Yorick are currently being pursued by THREE COWGIRLS ON HORSEBACK, all carrying rifles and wearing sheriff stars. The lead cowgirl is a Native American woman named TAD. Next to her is an angry white girl named JANE. And riding a beautiful black stallion is an African-American cowgirl named SONNY.

It's early afternoon now, and we're in the middle of a gorgeous open field. There are woods to either side of our riders, and we can see the Rocky Mountains in the background. Oh, and we should now be able to tell that Yorick is screaming with *excitement*, not fear.

Have fun with this, pardner!

3) Yorick: This is fucking *sweet*!

Page Five

Page Five, Panel One
Change angles for this profile shot of 355 and the hooded Yorick, on top of their speeding ATV.

1) Yorick: We're being chased by a *posse*!
2) Yorick: Of *cowgirls*!

3) Agent 355: Shut up, Yorick!

Page Five, Panel Two
Pull out to the largest panel of the page as we reveal that 355 is riding next to DR. MANN, who is awkwardly driving her own (smaller) ATV. She's wearing a helmet that covers much of her face.

4) Agent 355: Dr. Mann, keep up!

5) Dr. Mann: I'm trying, goddammit!
6) Dr. Mann: I learned how to drive this goddamn thing *yesterday*!

Page Five, Panel Three
Cut back to the pursuing cowgirls, as Tad orders the African-American Sonny to raise her rifle.

7) Tad: Sonny, take 'em!

Page Five, Panel Four
This is just a shot of Sonny, as she FIRES at the off-panel women she's pursuing.

8) SFX: *BLAM*

Page Six

Page Six, Panel One
Cut to the helmeted Dr. Mann, as one of the front tires of her ATV suddenly EXPLODES.

1) SFX: *SPAK*

Page Six, Panel Two
Change angles, as the ATV pitches forward and LAUNCHES Dr. Mann over its handlebars.

No Copy

Page Six, Panel Three
Change angles for this largest panel of the page. We're with the fallen and seemingly lifeless Dr. Mann in the extreme foreground of this shot. In the background, 355 breaks hard and brings the ATV screeching to a sideways halt. Yorick screams in horror.

2) Yorick: DOC!

Page Six, Panel Four
Push in on Yorick and 355, as they both hop off of the vehicle. We can see some dense woods in the immediate background. Yorick looks concerned, but 355 screams for him to get moving, while she starts to take the pet carrier off of the front of the ATV.

3) Agent 355: I'll take care of her! Go! Hide in the woods!

4) Yorick: But Ampersand—

5) Agent 355: I've got him, just *run* already!

Page Seven

Page Seven, Panel One
We're behind Agent 355 now, cheated so we can see some of her concerned expression. She's holding the pet carrier now, and she's approaching the unmoving Dr. Mann.

1) <u>Agent 355</u>: Dr. Mann?
2) <u>Agent 355</u>: *Allison*? Are you... ?

Page Seven, Panel Two
This is just a shot of the winded Dr. Mann, as she sits up and starts to remove her helmet.

3) <u>Dr. Mann</u>: I'm... I'm all right, 355.
4) <u>Dr. Mann</u>: I *told* you these dorky things save...

Page Seven, Panel Three
Pull out for this largest panel of the page. We're behind Dr. Mann here, as she finishes taking off her helmet (maybe she's still on one knee). Behind her, 355 has turned around to see what both women are now staring at: the super-posse. The three cowgirls have just stopped their horses in front of Mann and 355, and they have their rifles aimed at both women.

5) <u>Dr. Mann</u>: ... lives?

Page Seven, Panel Four
This is just a badass close-up of Tad, the Native American leader of these marshals.

6) <u>Tad</u>: Tell us where the third gal in your little raiding party went off to... or we start shooting more than *tires*.

Page Eight

Page Eight, Panel One
Change angles for this shot of 355 and the now-standing Dr. Mann. 355 holds up the sealed animal carrier as evidence, and Dr. Mann nervously tries to back up her friend's story.

1) <u>Agent 355</u>: I think your eyes were playing tricks on you, sheriff. There are only two of us, and we *aren't* here to steal your cattle.
2) <u>Agent 355</u>: We're trying to reach St. Joseph's Hospital in Denver so we can get some antibiotics for our *pet*.

3) <u>Dr. Mann</u>: He, uh, *she* got a bad cut on her arm a few days back, and I'm pretty sure it's *infected*. But if we had known this was private property—

Page Eight, Panel Two
Change angles for this shot of the three cowgirls, as they deftly DISMOUNT their horses.

4) <u>Jane</u>: Ain't nothing private about it. Land barons went extinct same time all the fellas did. This earth belongs to any woman wants to set foot on it.

5) <u>Sonny</u>: Any woman 'cept *Amazons*, that is.

Page Eight, Panel Three
Cut back to Dr. Mann and 355. Mann is visibly stunned by this accusation, while 355 uses her free hand to calmly reach inside of her jacket for something.

6) <u>Dr. Mann</u>: *Amazons*?

7) <u>Agent 355</u>: I'm afraid you're confused. I'm actually—

Page Eight, Panel Four
Change angles for this largest panel of the page, as Jane uses the butt of her rifle to SMASH 355 in the mouth.

8) Agent 355: Uhn!

Page Eight, Panel Five
This is just a menacing extreme close-up of 355, her gritted teeth now stained red with blood. She's trying her best not to hulk out.

9) Agent 355: That was... *unnecessary*.

Page Nine

Page Nine, Panel One
Pull out for this shot of 355 and the dubious Tad.

1) Agent 355: I was simply reaching for identification. I'm a *federal agent*.

2) Tad: Federal agent of *what*?

3) Agent 355: Technically, my organization is classified, but the President has authorized me to—

Page Nine, Panel Two
Cut over to Sonny and Jane, who both look impatient.

4) Sonny: Save that bullshit for the magistrates.

5) Jane: Yeah, we been warned about your kind... mutilatin' your own teats, tearing around on motorcycles, stealing food from defenseless women.

Page Nine, Panel Three
This is just a shot of Dr. Mann, screaming in protest.

6) Dr. Mann: You people have no *clue* what you're talking about!
7) Dr. Mann: We're *not* Daughters of the Amazon!

Page Nine, Panel Four
And this is just a close-up of Tad, as she matter-of-factly says:

8) Tad: Prove it.
9) Tad: Show us your breasts.

Page Nine, Panel Five
Pull out to this largest panel of the page for a group shot of Mann, 355 and the three cowgirls (who have all walked away from their off-panel horses).

10) Dr. Mann: *What*?

11) Tad: Relax, we're not homosexuals. Besides, if you're telling the truth, you ain't got nothing we haven't all seen—

12) Someone's Voice (from off): Reach for the sky, pardners!

Page Ten

Page Ten, Panel One
Change angles for this largest panel of the page, at least a half-SPLASH. We're

looking at the horses here, and we can now see that Yorick is standing next to the black stallion. He has a decent-sized BOWIE KNIFE pressed to the neck of the frightened animal. No longer wearing his hood, Yorick is now covering his mouth with a red bandana, bandit-style. He's holding the black horse hostage by its reins.

    1) <u>Yorick</u>: Or I turn Black Beauty here into a prop from *The Godfather*.

Page Ten, Panel Two
    Cut over to 355 and Mann. Mann looks baffled by this development, but 355 rolls her eyes knowingly.

    2) <u>Agent 355 (small, annoyed)</u>: Mother of Christ...

Page Ten, Panel Three
    Cut over to the three cowgirls. Tad is calmly formulating a plan, while Sonny screams in fear at the thought of something happening to her precious horse. Jane raises her rifle and aims it at the off-panel Yorick.

    3) <u>Sonny</u>: Buttercup!

    4) <u>Jane</u>: Butch, you so much as knick that horse, I kill you *and* your girlfriends.

Page Eleven

Page Eleven, Panel One
    This is just a shot of the bandana-clad Yorick.

    1) <u>Yorick</u>: What do I care?
    2) <u>Yorick</u>: We breastless Amazons *ache* for the sweet embrace of Mother Oblivion.

Page Eleven, Panel Two
    Cut back to the cowgirls. Jane and Tad look confused, but Sonny is still screaming in fear.

    3) <u>Jane</u>: Say *what*?

    4) <u>Tad</u>: Girl ain't right in the head.

    5) <u>Sonny</u>: Buttercup!

Page Eleven, Panel Three
    Cut back to Yorick, as he threatens to PLUNGE his knife into the throat of the captive steed.

    6) <u>Yorick</u>: Last chance, hand over your weapons to my associates.
    7) <u>Yorick</u>: Three... *two*...

Page Eleven, Panel Four
    Pull out to the largest panel of the page for a group shot of the whole crowd, as the three cowgirls reluctantly hand over their firearms to 355 and Dr. Mann (who looks extremely uncomfortable holding the two rifles she's just been handed). Tad keeps her eyes on Yorick as she relinquishes her weapon, while Jane curses under her breath.

    8) <u>Tad</u>: All right, all right!
    9) <u>Tad</u>: Just... just take her easy.

    10) <u>Jane (small, under her breath)</u>: Bitch.

Page Eleven, Panel Five
    This is just a kick-ass shot of 355, COCKING one of the old-fashioned rifles (by pulling down that lever-thing *underneath* the trigger). She looks hungry for revenge.

    11) <u>Agent 355</u>: Now then.

Page Twelve

Page Twelve, Panel One
Pull out to the largest panel of the page for this group shot. The cowgirls flinch as 355 FIRES the rifle... into the *air*. This causes the three horses to GALLOP AWAY at top speed.

    1) SFX: *BLAM*

Page Twelve, Panel Two
Change angles, as 355 starts to load Ampersand's carrying case and the rifles onto the ATV. Behind her, Jane looks confused.

    2) Agent 355: You've got about a two-hour walk back to civilization.
    3) Agent 355: I'll leave your weapons with the first reputable trading post we pass.

    4) Jane: You mean... you women *ain't* Amazons?

Page Twelve, Panel Three
We're behind Dr. Mann in the foreground of this shot, cheated so we can see some of her annoyed expression. We can clearly tell that she's opening her shirt to bare her breasts to the stunned cowgirls in the background, though we shouldn't actually *see* her Dr. Mammaries. (Sorry...)

    5) Dr. Mann: Do these look mutilated to you, you ignorant shitheads?

Page Twelve, Panel Four
This is just a small shot of Yorick (still wearing his bandana).

    6) Yorick (small, under his breath): Jeez.
    7) Yorick (small, under his breath): So much for protecting a lady's *dignity*...

Page Thirteen

Page Thirteen, Panel One
Cut to a few hours later for this page-wide, wide-angle establishing shot (the sun is starting to set in the distance). We can see our crew's ATV parked overlooking a cliff. 355, Mann and Yorick (standing around the vehicle) can just be tiny figures in this shot.

    No Copy

Page Thirteen, Panel Two
Push in on the trio for this largest panel of the page. On our left, Yorick is cradling an ailing Ampersand, who is howling in pain. Next to him, 355 is consulting a large foldout map of Colorado. Dr. Mann can be sitting on the parked ATV behind them.

    1) Ampersand: *oroooooo*

    2) Yorick: Jesus, I think Ampersand's getting worse, 355. Are we almost there?

    3) Agent 355: You're not going to the hospital, Yorick. Not after that crap you pulled back there.

Page Thirteen, Panel Three
Change angles for this shot of an indignant Yorick and 355, who calmly looks up from her map.

    4) Yorick: *What?* I save your lives, and you punish my *monkey*? He's gonna *die* without medicine!

    5) Agent 355: You didn't save our lives, you needlessly risked your own... *again*.

6) <u>Agent 355</u>: Anyway, Dr. Mann and I are still taking Ampersand to St. Joseph's. We're just not bringing *you* with us.

Page Thirteen, Panel Four
Change angles for this shot of Mann and 355, who are both looking at the off-panel Yorick.

7) <u>Dr. Mann</u>: If that Pony Express chick we met in Nebraska was telling the truth, St. Joe's is guarded like Area 51.
8) <u>Dr. Mann</u>: Getting my hands on more Augmentin is going to take patience, diplomacy and finesse.

9) <u>Agent 355</u>: Qualities you've never even *heard* of.

Page Thirteen, Panel Five
This is just a small shot of Yorick, looking genuinely worried.

10) <u>Yorick</u>: So you're... you're just going to *leave* me?

Page Fourteen

Page Fourteen, Panel One
Change angles for this shot of 355 and Mann, as 355 returns to her map.

1) <u>Agent 355</u>: Not by yourself.
2) <u>Agent 355</u>: I didn't want to do this, but I have a colleague who lives a few miles from here.

3) <u>Dr. Mann</u>: A Culper Ring agent?

Page Fourteen, Panel Two
Change angles for this shot of 355, and the now-pleading Yorick, still cradling his sickly pet.

4) <u>Agent 355</u>: *Ex*-Culper.
5) <u>Agent 355</u>: She took a permanent leave of absence after her husband-slash-partner was assassinated by *17 November*.

6) <u>Yorick</u>: Wait, I don't want to stay with some shell-shocked *widow*! Please! I promise, I'll be on my best behavior! I—

Page Fourteen, Panel Three
Similar framing, but now Yorick looks more skeptical than alarmed.

7) <u>Agent 355</u>: Yorick, I've known this woman since she was *nine*. We were in the same orphanage when we were both recruited.
8) <u>Agent 355</u>: Agent 711 has saved my ass almost as often as I've saved hers. You'll be fine.

9) <u>Yorick</u>: Hold on, her codename is seriously *711*? Man, how many guys used to ask if she's "open all night"?

Page Fourteen, Panel Four
This is just a close-up of Agent 355, looking deadly serious.

10) <u>Agent 355</u>: 711 was *General Washington's* codename during the Revolutionary War. That designation was awarded to my friend after she helped save the world from nuclear annihilation.
11) <u>Agent 355</u>: If you make a single crack at her expense, I will rip off your penis with a claw hammer.

Page Fourteen, Panel Five
Pull out for this largest panel of the page, as 355 walks towards us in the foreground. Behind her in the background, Yorick looks understandably nervous.

12) <u>Agent 355</u>: Saddle up.

Page Fifteen

Page Fifteen, Panel One
Cut to later that night (the sun has set now) for this page-wide establishing shot of a small cabin nestled in the woods of Colorado. We can see a woman sitting in a rocking chair on the porch, reading by the light of a Coleman gas lamp. We'll eventually learn that this is AGENT 711, a former Culper Ring operative in her late twenties (somewhat conservatively dressed). Maybe she can look like your original design for 355, Pia, back when she was a raven-haired white girl?

No Copy

Page Fifteen, Panel Two
Change angles for this largest panel of the page. We're with a stunned Agent 711 in the foreground of this shot, as she rises to greet the approaching Agent 355 and her two companions (Yorick is still holding Ampersand, and he has his hood up again).

1) <u>Agent 711</u>: Oh my god.
2) <u>Agent 711</u>: *355?*

3) <u>Agent 355</u>: Long time, 711.

Page Fifteen, Panel Three
Change angles, as 355 and 711 rush towards each other and EMBRACE.

No Copy

Page Fifteen, Panel Four
Similar framing, but now the two women pull apart and look at each other. Please leave some room between them for this rapid-fire exchange:

4) <u>Agent 711</u>: 1033?

5) <u>Agent 355</u>: He's dead. 241 and 853, too. *All* of the primes, obviously.

6) <u>Agent 711</u>: I can't imagine, 355. I'm still not over 1451.

Page Fifteen, Panel Five
Cut over to Dr. Mann and Yorick, who are eavesdropping on this bizarre dialogue.

7) <u>Dr. Mann</u>: We live in profoundly strange times.

8) <u>Yorick</u>: Yep.

Page Sixteen

Page Sixteen, Panel One
This is just a shot of 355, as she gestures at her off-panel friends.

1) <u>Agent 355</u>: 711, these are my new charges.
2) <u>Agent 355</u>: My *friends*.

Page Sixteen, Panel Two
Change angles, as 355 introduces 711 to Mann. 711 warmly shakes the doctor's

hand, but Mann just stares at her icily.

       3) <u>Agent 355</u>: Dr. Allison Mann, bioengineer out of Boston. If anyone can figure out what caused the Plague, it's *her*.

       4) <u>Agent 711</u>: Pleasure.

       5) <u>Dr. Mann</u>: Mn.

Page Sixteen, Panel Three
       Change angles again, as 355 introduces Yorick, who nonchalantly waves with his free hand (the one not cradling Ampersand).

       6) <u>Agent 355</u>: And this, as far as we know, is the last man on earth.

       7) <u>Yorick</u>: Hiya.

Page Sixteen, Panel Four
       Pull out to the largest panel of the page, as a floored 711 inspects the suddenly uncomfortable Yorick. 355 watches in the background.

       8) <u>Agent 711</u>: Is... is this some kind of *joke*?

       9) <u>Agent 355</u>: That's what I keep asking myself.

Page Sixteen, Panel Five
       Change angles for this shot of the two Culper agents, as 711 turns to talk with 355. Her question clearly makes 355 uneasy.

       10) <u>Agent 711</u>: *How*?
       11) <u>Agent 711</u>: Does... does this have something to do with the Amulet of *Helene*?

       12) <u>Agent 355</u>: Ah, actually, maybe we should speak in *private*, 711...

Page Seventeen

Page Seventeen, Panel One
       Pull out for this largest panel of the page. We're with Yorick and Mann in the fore-ground of this shot, as they watch 711 and 355 walk into the shadows in the background in order to speak in private.

       1) <u>Yorick</u>: Well, she seems... *nice*.

       2) <u>Dr. Mann</u>: I guess.
       3) <u>Dr. Mann</u>: Reminds me of one of my *exes*. Dumped me the night before my fucking MCAT.

Page Seventeen, Panel Two
       Change angles for this shot of an emotionless Dr. Mann and the puzzled Yorick. (I'm picturing these next four panels all being equal-sized page-wide letterbox shots, but as always, stick with what you think works best).

       4) <u>Yorick</u>: Hold on, *she* reminds you of an ex-*boyfriend*?

       5) <u>Dr. Mann</u>: That's not what I said.

       6) <u>Yorick</u>: Yes, you did! You just...

Page Seventeen, Panel Three
       Exact same framing, but now Yorick falls silent.

       No Copy

Page Seventeen, Panel Four
Exact same framing, but now Yorick's jaw drops as a light bulb goes off over his head. He shouldn't look disgusted, just surprised.

7) <u>Yorick</u>: Get out!
8) <u>Yorick</u>: You're telling me I've been traveling with you for a *year*, and I never even figured out that you were... you know...

Page Seventeen, Panel Five
Exact same framing one last time, as Mann and Yorick exchange two tiny (nearly imperceptible!) smiles.

9) <u>Dr. Mann</u>: Yes, well, I suppose we can add *gaydar* to the extraordinary number of common senses you seem to lack.

Page Eighteen

Page Eighteen, Panel One
Pull out to the largest panel of the page. We're with Mann and Yorick in the foreground of this shot, as they turn to see 355 and 711 walking out of the shadows in the background. 711 is now holding a small black journal.

1) <u>Agent 355</u>: All right, Doctor, I think we're ready to ride.
2) <u>Agent 355</u>: 711 has kindly offered to look after Yorick until we return.

Page Eighteen, Panel Two
Change angles for this shot of Yorick and Mann, as Yorick reluctantly hands the weary Ampersand over to the doctor.

3) <u>Yorick</u>: Come back with a healthy monkey, or don't come back at all.

4) <u>Dr. Mann</u>: Like you could live without me.

Page Eighteen, Panel Three
Change angles for this shot of 355 and Yorick, as she says goodbye to the suddenly troubled young man.

5) <u>Agent 355</u>: Be good, 'Rick.
6) <u>Agent 355</u>: I've left my journals with 711, just so she knows what she'll be dealing with.

7) <u>Yorick</u>: You... you keep a *journal*?

Page Eighteen, Panel Four
Change angles again, as Yorick and 711 watch their off-panel companions depart.

8) <u>Agent 711</u>: Why don't you come inside, Mr. Brown?

Page Eighteen, Panel Five
This is just an alluring close-up of 711, as she looks at us and arches an eyebrow.

9) <u>Agent 711</u>: I have something you might like to see.

Page Nineteen

Page Nineteen, Panel One
Cut to later that night for a different page-wide establishing shot of 711's cabin. There's smoke coming out of its small chimney here.

1) <u>From Cabin</u>: Holy crap!

Page Nineteen, Panel Two
Cut inside for this largest panel of the page. We're now inside of an expansive study that is lined from floor to ceiling with a billion and a half books. Yorick is awestruck by this sight, which makes his hostess smile. Yorick and 711 are both holding tea cups here.

2) Yorick: It's Paradise City!

3) Agent 711: They belonged to my husband. You're welcome to borrow as many as you like.

4) Yorick: You are a *goddess*. When I left Brooklyn, all I took with me was a copy of *Zen and the Art of Motorcycle Maintenance*. It's my girlfriend Beth's favorite book, but I have a short attention span for—

Page Nineteen, Panel Three
Change angles on the two, as Yorick suddenly notices a hardcover book on one of the shelves. He's pulling it out with a free hand here.

5) Yorick: Hey, *The Day of the Locust*!
6) Yorick: This is the greatest novel of all time!

7) Agent 711: Is that Nathaniel West? Never read him. I've always preferred *poetry* to prose.

Page Nineteen, Panel Four
Push in closer on the two, as Yorick looks down at the book. 711 is looking at him the way a therapist looks at a patient.

8) Yorick: Oh, it's got the most hilarious character ever, this guy named *Homer Simpson*.
9) Yorick (small, an aside): And this was written about fifty years before the cartoon, mind you.
10) Yorick: Homer's this awkward, naïve shut-in who's uncomfortable with his own sexuality. The book's about how he leaves his life of solitude to go to California.

11) Agent 711: And what does he hope to find there, Yorick?

Page Twenty

Page Twenty, Panel One
This is just a shot of Yorick, nervously talking as he sips from his teacup. Gulp, gulp, gulp...

1) Yorick: Huh? Oh, nothing, really. He just wants to *die*.
2) Yorick: I know that doesn't *sound* funny, but it is... and sad, and brilliant, and...

Page Twenty, Panel Two
Pull out to the largest panel of the page, as Yorick groggily lowers the teacup from his mouth. All of the color has drained from his face. 711 stares into the boy's half-mast eyes.

3) Yorick: ... and I... I think I'm gonna be *sick*.

4) Agent 711: No you're not, Yorick.
5) Agent 711: Just look into my eyes and listen to these words. You're familiar with *haiku*, aren't you... ?

Page Twenty, Panels Three through Seven
Okay, Pia, please don't get freaked out by the number of panels we have on this page! The next seven teen panels should all be literally the size of postage stamps in the final comic, so keep 'em small. We're essentially turning the lower 50% of this page into a graphic haiku. In this first tier, there are five panels, all with the same shot of 711's head from Yorick's P.O.V. 711 will say one word in each panel:

6) <u>Agent 711</u>: The

7) <u>Agent 711</u>: days

8) <u>Agent 711</u>: are

9) <u>Agent 711</u>: long

10) <u>Agent 711</u>: now

Page Twenty, Panels Eight through Fourteen
Second tier will have seven panels (again with one word in each), as 711's face becomes progressively more distorted.

11) <u>Agent 711</u>: Flies

12) <u>Agent 711</u>: born

13) <u>Agent 711</u>: in

14) <u>Agent 711</u>: shit

15) <u>Agent 711</u>: spread

16) <u>Agent 711</u>: new

17) <u>Agent 711</u>: wings

Page Twenty, Panels Fifteen through Nineteen
And this last tier will have five panels. 711's distorted face will get progressively darker, until we reach the final panel, which will be entirely **black**, and should ideally blend into this page's solid black background.

18) <u>Agent 711</u>: It's

19) <u>Agent 711</u>: your

20) <u>Agent 711</u>: turn

21) <u>Agent 711</u>: to

22) <u>Agent 711 (**tailless**)</u>: sleep

<u>Page Twenty-one</u>

Page Twenty-one, Panel One
Cut to an hour later for this close-up of an exhausted Yorick, as he struggles to open one eye. A little drool is coming out of his mouth. We're not playing this for laughs, so Yorick should look genuinely *awful*.

1) <u>Yorick (small, groggy)</u>: Ghh.

Page Twenty-one, Panel Two
Okay, Clem, lettered into the center of this black panel is white text, but instead of a location caption, it's this line of dialogue (which should be in the same font/size as our standard location captions):

2) <u>White text on black background</u>:
Yorick, you need to wake up.

Page Twenty-one, Panel Three
Pull out to this largest panel of the page, at least a half-SPLASH. We're in some kind of dark, dank cellar now, where Yorick is trussed in the most elaborate Japanese rope bondage set-up in the history of the art. All of the reference you found is amazing, Pia, but I particularly liked the ones where the subject is completely suspended over the floor (though

Yorick's head should be pulled back so that it's looking at "us" here). Either way, he should be completely naked, with his genitals covered by shadows or ropes (as I don't think we can get away with full-frontal male nudity). Again, this needs to be shocking and unpleasant.

3) <u>Yorick (small, groggy)</u>: Loud... so loud in my *head*...

4) <u>Someone's Voice (from off)</u>: Shut your fucking *mouth*, jester. The fun and games are over...

Page Twenty-two

Page Twenty-two, SPLASH
Cut over to the entrance of this cellar for this three-quarter SPLASH (please leave some negative space at the bottom of our page for the credits and title). Standing here is Agent 711, who's now wearing an extraordinary DOMINATRIX OUTFIT (this should be a nice full-figure shot, thigh-high boots and all). Go with whatever leather/latex/etc. floats your boat, Pia, but I really think we should put her in one of those underwire push-up bustiers that leaves the breasts exposed, since we've held off showing any female nudity until now, and this is certainly the moment to make it count. Either way, 711 should also be holding a whip (or some instrument of torture), and she looks like she could dish out more punishment than any one man could survive. Keeping with our darker shift in tone, 711 should *not* be smiling here. Instead, her expression is stern and determined.

1) <u>Agent 711</u>: It's time to get serious.

2) <u>Title</u>:

Safeword
chapter one

3) <u>Credits</u>:

Brian K. Vaughan Pia Guerra
Writer/Co-creators/Penciller

José Marzán, Jr.
Inker

Clem Robins
Letterer

Pamela Rambo
Colorist

Digital Chameleon
Separations(?)

J.G. Jones
Cover Artist

Zachary Rau
Assistant Editor

Will Dennis
Editor

Y: The Last Man Created by Brian K. Vaughan and Pia Guerra